THE BOY FROM ATLANTIS

Knight Jordan

KNIGHT PRODUCTION, LLC

First Edition: 2020
ISBN: 978-1-7357596-0-9

Cover Art by the Ridenour Brothers
Pencils & Inks by Aaron Ridenour
Colors & Lettering by Brian Ridenour

Story Consultation by Megan Jean Jordan
Edited by Rachel@fantasyediting.com
Formatting Consulting by Kevin Mellander

Printed in the United States of America

For Molly, Kate, Nic, Brooks, Megan, Ian and Kenzie.
I love you family!

Special Thanks to Mego for starting this project, and always believing
in me.

And Kenzie, who made me a ceramic The Boy From Atlantis jar,
and asked almost daily when the book would be finished.

Chapter 1
The Inciting Incident

I looked up at the ornate, majestic throne; towering in front me. Above the throne was a protective, transparent dome covered the entire coronation room, truly a magnificent site to behold.

The spectacular bioluminescent of the deep sea surround the dome and illuminated the entire room. Brilliant effervescent blue, green and white lights danced overhead. Beyond the dome, various species of deep sea fish darted in and out of view, and a squid majestically glided passed the side of the dome.

I looked at my reflection in the dome and saw a handsome, young man who is ready to lead his people.

Too young to rule they said. Ha! I'd show them. My pedigree and prestigious education had prepared me for this moment. Tomorrow would be a day of triumph and celebration.

I took a deep breath and smiled at my reflection. Looking past the dome I saw what resembled large fish, headed toward him. Stupid creature better slow down or it will smash right into the dome. I squinted to see more clearly. Why is it still racing toward me?

The closer the object came I realized it wasn't a fish, but a reflection of a shadowy figure swiftly coming up behind me.

Puzzled, I turned around.

Crack! A thick metal bar smashed into the slide of my head. My body went limp and crashed on the floor, the back of head slammed against the cold, marble surface.

Pain shot through my whole body. A kaleidoscope of colors danced in front of my eyes. I clutched my head and screamed.

"Ahhhh! Guards, help…" Blood streamed down my forehead. The room started to spin and my vision went out of focus, fading in and out of black.

Consumed with agony, I was barely aware that my ankles were being tightly gripped by a pair of rough hands. The villain dragged me across the room, intensifying the excruciating pain, as my head bounced off the floor.

The green and blue colors that surrounded me blurred. My skull felt like it had been split in two. Through cloudy vision I watched helpless while my assailant mercilessly pulled me toward what looked like a large frameless glass wall, the dome.

"Stop!" I shouted

The figure standing by me feet pointed at the dome. It was too dark, and my vision to blurred to make out who this was. Without warning I was grabbed by my arms and pulled up to almost a standing position. Before I could look to the side and see who was holding me, I was launched head first at the dome. I closed my eyes, and felt my body pass through the thick, damp barricade of the dome and into the surrounding dark water.

I looked back at the dome and saw the silhouette of the cowards who attacked me. Three figures stood inside the dome like statues. In unison they turned and walked away, fading out of sight.

Floating in the water I tried to process what had just happened. Why was this happening to me? Who were they? The intense pain in my head was preventing forming coherent thoughts.

Still dazed, I began to slowly swim toward the dome. I had drifted about twenty feet away, and in my weaken state I struggled to make it back.

Out of the darkness, a violent, whirling mass of water suddenly caught up. I frantically swung my arms around and kicked my feet. The vortex was overpowering. It sucked me in and clasped my body with such force that I gasped for air. Salty water filled my lungs, causing an intense burning. My chest felt like it was going to explode.

The cocoon of water began to crush me. I knew that within moments my ribs would snap. Any air left in my lungs was being forced out.

Breathe. A flash of insight raced in and out of my mind. Yes, I could breathe in water.

I attempted to relax and let instincts take over but the pressure around me increased, and I was dragged farther down into the depths of the ocean. There was no escaping this imminent death.

With a desperate choking cry for help, more water gushed down my throat. I closed my eyes and waited for the inevitable.

Chapter 2
Fish Out of Water

Everything around me was dark. My body lay prostrate on a moist, granular surface. I stretched out a tentative hand and explored the area around. I felt something cold, wet, and gritty. Sand, why was I on sand?

With some effort I managed to roll over on my side. I coughed and spit up several chunks of sand before flopping onto my back. I gently stroked my throat, it was so sore.

What am I doing here? I stared up at the night sky. Every muscle still ached, as if I had been swimming for days. Yes, swimming. I remember being in the ocean.

As I became more cognizant, I realized waves were lapping at my toes. I lifted my head and looked down at my feet. It was too dark to really see much, but the sound of the waves and feeling of the water brought a tranquil feeling of peace.

I rested my head back on the sand and closed my eyes. Pictures of a strange, yet magnificent city and water, lots and lots of water, passed through my mind. I couldn't discern what I was seeing. I furrowed my brow as I attempted to concentrate and make sense of all the images I was seeing; a fragment of memories was my best guess.

Suddenly a searing pain erupted in my head and my mind went blank, literally, all the imagines vanished and I only saw black. I clutched my head with both hands and moaned. After a few intense moments the pain became a dull throbbing and I slowly opened my eyes.

Exerting what little energy I had, I forced myself to stand. My legs shook and wobbled like jelly. I took one shaky step forward and both my knees buckled. Frustrated, I fell onto the rough sand.

Get up now! Determined, but still struggling, I raised up again. After swaying back and forth for a moment, I managed to establish my equilibrium.

Standing erect, I squinted into the darkness. The moonlight revealed an expanse of endless sand and rock that eventually crawled away into the thick fog.

Through the fog and mist, I saw a glowing object far in the distance and high above the sand and rock. I began to walk in its direction.

With each step I felt a strange sensation in my feet. Something was stuck between my toes. I had the same feeling on my hands; a sticky substance was between my fingers.

I held up my hand toward the moon; its brightness illuminated a thin film of skin that stretched between each of my digits. *What is this?* I put both hands in front of me and I stared at them in shock.

Chapter 2
Fish Out of Water

Everything around me was dark. My body lay prostrate on a moist, granular surface. I stretched out a tentative hand and explored the area around. I felt something cold, wet, and gritty. Sand, why was I on sand?

With some effort I managed to roll over on my side. I coughed and spit up several chunks of sand before flopping onto my back. I gently stroked my throat, it was so sore.

What am I doing here? I stared up at the night sky. Every muscle still ached, as if I had been swimming for days. Yes, swimming. I remember being in the ocean.

As I became more cognizant, I realized waves were lapping at my toes. I lifted my head and looked down at my feet. It was too dark to really see much, but the sound of the waves and feeling of the water brought a tranquil feeling of peace.

I rested my head back on the sand and closed my eyes. Pictures of a strange, yet magnificent city and water, lots and lots of water, passed through my mind. I couldn't discern what I was seeing. I furrowed my brow as I attempted to concentrate and make sense of all the images I was seeing; a fragment of memories was my best guess.

Suddenly a searing pain erupted in my head and my mind went blank, literally, all the imagines vanished and I only saw black. I clutched my head with both hands and moaned. After a few intense moments the pain became a dull throbbing and I slowly opened my eyes.

Exerting what little energy I had, I forced myself to stand. My legs shook and wobbled like jelly. I took one shaky step forward and both my knees buckled. Frustrated, I fell onto the rough sand.

Get up now! Determined, but still struggling, I raised up again. After swaying back and forth for a moment, I managed to establish my equilibrium.

Standing erect, I squinted into the darkness. The moonlight revealed an expanse of endless sand and rock that eventually crawled away into the thick fog.

Through the fog and mist, I saw a glowing object far in the distance and high above the sand and rock. I began to walk in its direction.

With each step I felt a strange sensation in my feet. Something was stuck between my toes. I had the same feeling on my hands; a sticky substance was between my fingers.

I held up my hand toward the moon; its brightness illuminated a thin film of skin that stretched between each of my digits. *What is this?* I put both hands in front of me and I stared at them in shock.

From seemingly out of nowhere, a brilliant beam of light shot across the sky; it made the moon seem dull in comparison. The beam swung out over the turbulent waters and danced across the crests of the waves. I stared in awe.

I didn't know if I was more perplexed with the strange growth between my fingers and toes, or this magical funnel of light that dominated the night sky.

My eyes followed the beam of light from its position hovering over the water, and back to the shore line. I discovered a beam of light emitting from a large, glowing cylinder, on the rocky shore line. The stream of light protruding from its top swung back and forth over the mass of dark water.

I continued walking toward the source of this mesmerizing light, but abruptly halted, seeing something moving in the fog.

My heart began to race and fear gripped me when a shadowy figure emerged. I stood frozen in my tracks. It made a deep growling sound. I was certain my life was in peril.

Chapter 3
Stranger Danger

Ouch! A stabbing pain ripped across my skull. My brain was translating the sound I was hearing. It was as if a switch had been turned on inside my brain. The unintelligible noise from the fog became a voice.

"Who's out there?" A deep voice bellowed.

From about thirty feet away, an old man stepped out from the fog. His skin was dark and his beard and hair were white, almost silver. He took something from off his head. I knew the word; a helmet, no, a tunic, no, hat...cap. He was waving his cap at me.

This was not a threat, I sensed that now. I knew the language of origin wasn't my own, but somehow I was able to understand it. The old man continued to walk toward me.

I lifted my hand to return his gesture, but then I remembered my strange skin condition. Quickly I held my arms tight to my side and stared straight ahead.

Maybe my condition wasn't so strange; maybe this man and I were the same type of... of whatever I was.

"Who is that?" he shouted.

I swallowed hard and attempted to respond, but I couldn't utter a sound.

"Are you alright?" the old man was now ten feet from me.

Without warning streaks of light flashed overhead. Caught off guard, I stumbled. My equilibrium failed me and I toppled to the side. The old man caught me in his arms, just before I hit the sand. His big brown eyes showed deep concern. My feelings of fear dissipated; this man could be a potential ally.

"Are you okay son?" the man inquired. I stared blankly at him. "What's your name?" he continued.

My mind was blank. I didn't know how to answer him.

Rain pelted my face. With a blank stare, I just kept looking up at him.

Not knowing how else to communicate, I shook my head. The sudden motion caused the world around me to spin, my body went limp, my eyes rolled back and then, once again, there was nothing but darkness.

Chapter 4
Pleasant Awakening

Pain! Water! Brilliant flashes of light! Rapid images crashed through my mind. I couldn't comprehend what I was seeing. Choking! I was drowning. *Somebody help me!*

I shook my head back and forth. My arms and legs twitched. Suddenly my eyes popped open. Anxiously, I felt the area around me. The gritty sand had been replaced by a soft surface. Comfortable warmth was draped over my prostrate body. I was relieved to discover it was only a lucid dream. Yet, I still feared the worst.

A blue sky with large billowing clouds floated above me. Perhaps I was still dreaming?

After a few moments, I realized the clouds were not moving or changing shape. I was looking at the walls and ceiling of a curve-shaped room. Where was I?

"Well, good morning, young man," came a soft voice.

This was not the same deep voice I remembered from my dark night encounter. This voice was sweet and pleasant. I scrunched my eye lids and blinked several times. Once my eyes focused, I discovered a petite elderly lady standing by me feet.

The sunlight coming through the window surrounded her, giving the little lady a sublime glow. She too had white hair and brown skin like the man I encountered on the beach. Kind eyes, I will never forget those kind eyes, looked down at me.

My mind tried to switch into a defensive mode, but it couldn't. Her tender voice caused my brow to unfurl and I released a breath of relief. My eyes widen and I gave a slight smile. I had become quite docile.

"My name is Mary Starr," the elderly lady said softly. "We hope you slept well."

Just then the old man from the fog poked his head in the doorway.

"So, he's awake." The man scratched his curly beard. "Did you get a name outta him yet?"

"Hush, dear," Mary Starr said. "He's obviously been through a lot."

The old man enthusiastically sniffed the air then clapped his hands together.

"Time to turn over the cakes," he exclaimed, before he briskly exited.

Mary gave me a smile and a wink. I admit I wasn't sure why, but I since she kept looking at me so I thought it best to return the gesture. My attempt to mimic her action only produced an awkward squint. She walked around the side of structure I was laying on and came over to my side. Still smiling, she gently put her hand on my shoulder. I flinched, but ever so slightly. Mary's hand remained, and she gave me a soft, reassuring pat.

"Of course, you've already met my husband Roger."

I gave a slight nod of acknowledgement.

"And you are?" Mary paused, waiting for my reply.

I am... I am... Who am I? I could not make my mouth form the words my brain was telling me to say.

Not only was I unable to speak her language, I wasn't remembering; I didn't know who I was, where I was, or how I got here. A sick feeling came over me. My breathing became heavier and I nervously scanned my surrounding. All I could give Mary was a tense shoulder shrug and look of confusion. She softly squeezed my shoulder.

"Everything is going to be alright."

I should have felt more afraid, but Mary's gentle voice and comforting touch had a calming effect on me. I still felt a little anxiety though; being in such unfamiliar surroundings, with a fractured memory. I say fractured, because I could identify general things like a door, a window and even the soft bed I was laying on, but I couldn't recall my name, or the language I spoke.

Mary removed her hand from my shoulder and picked something off the ground.

"You had these on when Roger found you."

She held out her arms and presented me with some shiny articles of clothing. I nodded and accepted a pair of metallic looking blue shorts and an equally metallic red shirt. Both had golden trim along the edges.

Mary cleared her throat. "I must say, I've never seen an outfit quite like this before. I don't recognize the fabric at all."

I ran my hand over the clothes. Honestly, I couldn't remember wearing them, but I was glad I was found wearing something. I looked up at Mary and shrugged again. She smiled.

"Not to worry, let me help you up dear."

My hands! I had almost forgotten my discovery of the preceding evening. It was too late; Mary had pulled back the blanket.

Relieved, I found no signs of extra skin between my fingers. My hands had the same appearance as Mary's, well perhaps a little less wrinkled and not as dark.

She took my hands and gently pulled me up. Looking down, I was again relieved that my feet were void of any sticky, superfluous flesh.

The pants I was wearing had little sail boats on them. This caused me to smile and I rubbed the soft material between my fingers. It felt a bit strange, but nice.

"Roger had an extra pair of pajamas he was willing to part with. Sorry, they may be a little baggy," Mary said apologetically. "You clothes are dry now, and you're welcome to change back into them."

I patted my sail boat pants and smiled again. The material that covered me was fuzzy and comfortable. My top even matched my pants. I wanted to keep my baggy, blue outfit on.

A slight twinge of pain manifested in my head. Thoughts and words were formulating and processing.

My mind was telling me to say the words "thank you", but again my mouth still was not able to articulate my brain's request.

Sorry Mary, hopefully soon I'll be able to express my gratitude.

Chapter 5
Mouth Watering

Without soliciting a response, Mary took me by the arm and assisted me down a narrow hallway. After a few steps, we entered another round shaped room. So many shinny objects; there were silver containers with black handles sitting on top of a raised platform, a rectangle sliver object with two grooves in it and a large, silver sudden container with a curved shinny pipe protruding from it.

Roger was also in the room. His back was to us and he was singing something while standing in front a box that had a flame coming out its top. I could tell what he was doing but his arms were moving in a circular motion.

In the middle of the room was a big, flat round object, suspended in the air by four posts. On top of the flat object were a container full of colorful objects; some red and round, some green and oval, and a few yellow, slender and curved.

"My sanctuary of indulgence," Mary said, sniffing the air.

I cock my head to one side and gave Mary and puzzled look. She smile and motioned for me to move toward the round object.

"You had quite a night it would seem. Better get something inside you."

Mary pulled out a chair and I sat at the table. *Yes, I remember the word, table!*

I looked at the table and tapped my fingers on it. A delicious scent drifted towards me. The inside of my mouth moistened. I smacked my lips together and my stomach produced an odd noise.

"Sounds like something's about to burst." Roger said, placing a round white disk in front of me. He and Mary took their seats at the table. I just starred at the offering before me.

On top of the disk were round objects covered in a golden liquid. A small yellow square lay on top of the objects. The little square seemed to be shrinking and streams of the square were merging with the flowing golden liquid.

Mary gently placed a prong shaped stick in my hand. This item actually felt strangely familiar to me, but for some reason I thought it should have been much larger. I held the instrument up and looked down at the steaming objects before me.

"You waitin' for an invitation?" Roger muttered.

His comment made me smile, and I wasn't even sure why. Perhaps it was his delivery.

"Eat up son," he ordered.

I carefully and instinctively placed a small piece of the thick, steamy circle into my mouth. Wow! The sensations I experienced were indescribable. Warmth, joy, excitement and anticipation all rolled into one amazing feeling.

"Is it okay?" Mary sat across from me waiting for a response. Roger put his arm around her shoulders. He leaned toward me and his eyes opened wide. He seemed equally as anxious for a response.

I wanted to exclaim, "This isn't okay, It's FREAKIN' FANTASTIC!"

Sadly, I still couldn't produce any of these words. *Why wasn't my mouth cooperating with what my brain was telling it would have been an appropriate phrase in this situation?*

I stretched my mouth as wide as I could, with lips together of course, I didn't want any of this amazing substance to escape.

My goofy grin caused Mary and Roger to looked at each other laugh. Roger kissed Mary on the cheek.

"He loves it," Roger said, lovingly squeezing Mary's shoulder.

"Who wouldn't?" Roger smiled to himself.

Mary held up a piece of cloth and pointed at my mouth. I reached up with my hand, but Mary intercepted, and placed the cloth in my hand. She guided my hand careful wiped some escaping food from off my chin. I stared at the cloth wondering why Mary felt the need to take excess food from my face.

Mary told me it was a napkin, and should be used generously. Her instruction was informative and not condescending. I knew that she really wanting me to understand the environment I was in. We exchanged pleasant glances.

Sitting around the table with this elderly couple felt nice, it felt peaceful, and it felt good.

Chapter 6
No Place Like A Home

Over the course of this amazing meal, Mary and Roger explained to me that I was in their home, a home they had occupied for many, many years. They told me that they were the keepers of the light house. I smiled and nodded my head, even though I really didn't completely understand what they were saying.

Mary stood up and went over to the large upright box in the corner of the room. The same box she had previously taken the orange liquid I was now drinking and enjoying.

She pulled a small, rectangular, flat item off the front of the large, white box and brought it to me. It was a picture. She pointed at the picture and identified the objects on it as their "home" and the "lighthouse".

I nodded, this time with enthusiasm.

That's what I saw last night, the lighthouse. It was magnificent. I looked around the room and then pointed to the picture of the house.

"Yes," Mary said. "We are in this house right now. And attached to our home is the lighthouse."

My eyes widened and I sat up straight. This I had to see for myself. I stood up from the table. Mary smiled and nodded.

"Huh," Roger said. "Bit strange, ain't he?"

"Manners Mr. Starr," Mary scowled. "That is just plain rude."

"Sweetheart," Roger said, "It's not like he can understand me."

I could hear their words, but I didn't grasp the meaning. I gathered by Mary's reaction that the word "strange" wasn't very complimentary. I gave Roger a smile.

Noticing a small window in the kitchen, I walked over to it and peered through. I was hoping to once again see the magnificent lighthouse we were supposed to be adjacent to.

I titled my head, and saw a white, rounded, stone like surface. I think it was the side of the lighthouse, but I couldn't be sure.

Roger walked up beside me and placed his rough, wrinkled hand on my shoulder.

"If you want a real look, come with me."

Roger escorted me to the front door. He motioned for me to put on some foot coverings, like what he had on. I looked at the coverings and back at Roger's covered feet.

"Don't be shy, just slip your feet right on in them boots."

I attempted to hop both feet into the "boots" but lost my balance and crashed to the floor. After some laughter Roger helped me up and instructed me on the proper protocol for applying one's footwear.

"Very fashionable dear," Mary teased. "Pajamas and rubber boots."

Roger scoffed. "It's not like the neighbors are gonna' see him."

Mary shook her head, and Roger gave her a huge grin.

"Come on," Roger instructed me.

Hoping Mary would be joining us, I looked back over my shoulder. I found her company to be a sweet balance to Roger's brash approach.

"Not a chance kid," Roger must have read my mind. "Mrs. Starr has climbed them stairs more than her fair share." Mary gave Roger a loving smile. "It'll just be us fellas."

We left Mary inside her home, and Roger and I walked on a small, worn stone path that led to the base of the lighthouse. I looked up at the tall white cylinder in front of me I awe. I have a reverent respect for this structure; it led me into the safe, caring arms of the man I now knew as Roger Starr.

Chapter 7
The Lighthouse

Roger spoke with enthusiasm while we made our ascent on what felt like an endless spiral staircase.

"Lighthouses have been around since ancient Egypt you know."

I didn't know what Egypt was, let alone the history of lighthouses.

"In fact, the oldest functioning lighthouse in the world is in north Spain."

My tour guide was a wealth of knowledge regarding the maritime. I enjoyed listening to Roger; it made the climb up the unyielding staircase more enjoyable. Were we ever going to reach our destination?

"Then there was that famous Scottish family, the huh... let's see, the Stevenson Family."

Roger managed to continue pontificating without losing his breath. I was breathing quiet heaving and took advantage of the use of the hand railing to pull myself up the steps.

"They built gobs of lighthouses along the coastline of Scotland." Roger continued, "Yet no two lighthouses have been built the same. We're one of the few manned lighthouses in existence. Most are automated now. We like to keep things simple around these parts."

Roger looked back at me for a reaction. I simple raised my eyebrows, hoping to convey an expression of wonder. Roger smiled and stopped at the top of the stairs.

"Well, here we are." He pushed open a heavy metal door.

I stepped through the door, and immediately stopped. What I saw was amazing. We were surrounded by transparent walls. I could see far into the distance from this majestic high tower. Tiny houses, like the Starrs' home, dotted the landscape. These houses were square in shape though, so not exactly like the one below me.

Roger took hold of my arm and guided me around the lighthouse's "lantern". He said it is the heart of the lighthouse. Round the lantern I was introduced to a most spectacular view. The scene literally caused my jaw to drop. Rays from the rising sun sparkled and shimmered across an endless body of water.

Standing there with my mouth wide open I was aware of Roger in the background still taking. He was explaining the advancements for lighthouses, such as automated time clocks and Fresnel lenses.

Fascinating to say the least; however, I could not take my eyes off the immense ocean that stretched across the horizon, I was transfixed.

Roger kept explaining the various intricacies of the lighthouse and I kept looking out at the ocean.

I had a strange, yet distinct feeling that someone or something was watching me from afar. I squinted and moved closer to the glass window.

The watcher was out there, somewhere in the horizon, I just knew. By squinting harder I hoped somehow to improve my vision. I still could not see anything but a few sailboats and lots of water.

The more I looked the more the feeling of being watched intensified. I felt the horizon its self was reaching out for me.

Without warning a sharp, intense, stabbing pain slammed around inside my skull. Images of angry faces and swirling water flashed before my eyes. The pain increased and I dropped to one knee.

"You all right lad?" Roger lifted me back to me feet. "The altitude up here ain't for everyone."

I nodded in agreement.

"I'll help you down the stairs," Roger continued.

"Ready," Roger said. He walked carefully in front of me and I put one hand on the railing and the other on his shoulder, per his request.

Descending the winding stairs seemed just as long, if not longer than our journey up them. With each step my head pounded. Suddenly everything around me became fuzzy and then everything went completely dark.

Chapter 8
Failure to Communicate

I forced my eyes open, and through blurred vision saw three figures standing over me. I was laying on what the Starrs called the sofa; well, Mary called it a sofa, and Roger called it a couch; either way it was very comfortable to me.

Hoping to improve my sight, I squeezed my eyes tight and then blinked several times. With my surrounding in focus, I saw Roger, Mary and a lady in a long white coat. I shook my head and blinked again.

"Well hello there," said the lady.

I tilted my head and gave her a smile.

Mary put her arm around the lady's waist. "This is Doctor Groves. We thought it best to have you checked out."

"These black outs you're havin' got us concerned," Roger said.

Doctor Groves reached down and put her hand on my shoulder. "You're going to be alright Kyle." Doctor Groves stood back up and addressed Mary. "Your nephew is definitely dehydrated. He will need plenty of water. Tylenol or Advil should take care of that ear infection."

Mary squeezed the doctor's arm. "Thanks Barb."

Doctor Groves looked down at me.

"Kyle, if this happens again, you come see me. Okay?"

I smiled and gave the Doctor a nod, even though I wasn't quite sure what I was agreeing to do.

Mary and Roger walked out of the room with the doctor. I stayed on the sofa-couch admiring the soft multi-colored large piece of material that was covering my prone body. Apparently I had rested here for most of the day.

"Here you go Kyle." Roger handed me a glass of water.

Smiling graciously, I accepted and drank it down in one gulp, then motioned to Roger, more please.

Roger chuckled, "Does a body good."

"You gave us quite a scare, young man," came Mary's voice from the other side of the sofa-couch.

Mary looked so sad, her eyes were wet. I clenched my teeth together and widened my eyes, hoping to convey a sincere apology. Mary gently touched my shoulder.

"You just relax now, we'll be right over here".

Mary walked over to a square box that was on top of a table. Ha! I knew the word table. My brief time at the "kitchen table" had paid off. Good for me.

Roger watched Mary walk away. He turned to me and gave a sigh.

"Mary ain't found of lying and all; in fact, we actually use a fancier word for it, suppose it lessen the guilt"

I scrunched my forehead. Roger smiled. "We told the Doc you are our nephew."

I looked at Roger blankly.

"Anyhow, you just rest a spell."

I shrugged and Roger accompanied Mary at their machine.

I probably should have been excited by all the words and pictures that were appearing before them, but since I didn't remember seeing anything like it before, I wasn't able to decipher their written language. I just felt more confused.

I wished so much that I could translate the words that kept materializing on their box. Why could I understand when Mary and Roger spoke words, but all their written language was just a jumble of symbols?

Mary told me they were looking at missing persons websites and police news reports. This task seemed somewhat frustrating for Roger, who constantly complained about the speed of the machine. My presence seemed to be making them uncomfortable, because they kept looking back over their shoulders at me and manufacturing forced smiles. I decided to go to my designated room and give them some privacy.

Roger's hand-me-downs lay at the foot of the bed. I tried some on for size and stood in front of a tall, flat shiny object. *"Come on, I should know the name of this item."*

It was as if I was looking into a calm pool of water. I didn't recognize the lean, yet fit looking, young boy with bright blue eyes and thick black hair looking back at me. Was this really who I was?

I empathized with the frustration Roger and Mary were feeling regarding my inability to answer their questions about my origin. "How old are you?", "Where are your parents?", "Where did you come from?" and of course the ever popular, "What is your name?"

I hated causing these kind people such anguish. I wanted so badly to be able to respond to their inquiries, but what would I have said; I didn't know how or why I ended up alone on the shore in the middle of the night.

Looking out the little window of my designated room, I watched the setting sun's reflection dance across the ocean's blue blanket of water. The night sky filled with flickering stars.

Since my hosts were otherwise engaged with their "internet" searching, I decided to venture outside on my own. I wanted to get a better look at the stars and the ocean. I couldn't explain it, but I felt a definite connection to that vast body of soft liquid.

Chapter 9
Lost Starr

Mary and Roger didn't look up when I passed by the room they were sitting in, so I quietly made my way down a narrow hallway.

After opening several locked doors, I eventually found the one leading outside.

It felt good to be outside the Starr's dwelling. A feeling of peace came over me as I breathed in the cool, salty night air.

Without hesitation, I walked down a well-worn path to the edge of a cliff that overlooked the ocean.

What a magnificent sight at night. The air was crisp and fresh. My body swayed as I watched the endless water dance under the star filled sky.

The crashing waves sounded like voices, voices beckoning me to reunite with the water. I was in a tranquil state, until a strange sensation came over me, a sensation of being watched. It was the same feeling I had in the lighthouse; somewhere in the far distance, someone or something was watching me.

Needing to get a better look, I squinted and stepped close to the edge of the cliff.

"Get back!" Mary's shrill voice crashed through the night air.

I spun around to see her and knocked a few loose stones off the cliff with my foot. Curious, I looked back over my shoulder and watched the little rocks plop in the dark water below.

"No!" Mary's scream was even louder the second time.

She ran toward me with her arms flailing. Fear gripped me and I stood still.

My heart pounded furiously and the images around me started to spin. That sharp, stabbing pain that had plagued returned. The pounding inside my skull intensified.

The next thing I knew I was laying on the ground with my head cradled in Mary's lap. Her tears fell on my face and rolled down my cheek. Seeing this tender, loving woman cry caused a swell of emotion inside of me. My eyes became full of salty discharge.

"Not again," cried Mary. "Not again." She rocked me gently in her arms and looked up at the sky. "Please Jeremy, please stay with me."

Jeremy? Was that someone or something in the stars? Mary said the name again, this time looking deep into my eyes. Impulsively I reached up and touched her soft wrinkled face. I wanted so badly to communicate with her and tell her that everything was okay. I attempted to utter the word "sorry", but all that came out was an "ah" sound.

Soon, Roger was by her side. He helped both of us off the ground. Mary nuzzled her face into Roger's shoulder and shook her head. I swallowed hard, knowing that I had been the cause of Mary's pain and tears.

The wind picked up and we all shivered as we made our way back to the little round dwelling nestled at the bottom of the lighthouse.

Back in the warmth of the house, Mary and Roger sat me down on the sofa-couch. The conversation began with the usual, "We don't know if you can understand what we are saying, but we think you do. Well, at least we hope you can." I responded with my customary smile and nod.

Roger and Mary proceeded to tell me about a son they had. He heroically attempted to save a little girl who had fallen off the side of the cliff into the unforgiving waters below.

Roger did most of the talking. Their son was unfortunately unsuccessful in his rescue efforts. He and the child "lost" their lives. "Lost" their lives? The word lost didn't make sense to me. Couldn't anything that was "lost" be found?

Mary produced a photo album containing numerous pictures of their son. Even though the color of our bodies looked different, and his head consisted of circles of hair; they said their son and I had the exact same smile and a twinkle of curiosity in our eyes.

Mary and Roger left me alone to flip through the pages of their treasured book. With each picture I viewed, a gentle, warm feeling grew inside of me. I knew this family shared great love for each other.

This time the tears in my eyes were not from fear, guilt or sadness, but from joy. Their book radiated joy. I wondered if I would ever belong to such joy.

With tear-filled eyes I walked into the kitchen. Roger and Mary were sitting in silence. Upon seeing me, Mary immediately rose and enveloped me in her arms. Peace returned to my heart, the same peace I had felt when I watched the ocean move with all its power and majesty.

Chapter 10
Tutelage via TV

Several days passed and my routine became very predictable. When the sun came up at 6a.m., I would awaken. Sadly, the nightmares of swirling water and shadowed, angry faces were the things I remembered when I opened my eyes to start the day.

My nerves were always calmed when I became cognizant enough to realize I was still in my soft bed; covered by equally soft, comforting sheets and blankets.

I would stay in bed until the sweet aroma of Mary's breakfast drifted down the hallway and into my room. Breakfast was delicious as always. After my meal I listened to a stimulating conversation between Roger and Mary, with the occasional nods and smiles sent in my direction. I was soon invited to retired to the sofa-couch. Once there I was positioned in front of a large rectangle, they called the "teley".

The next few hours were spent "channel surfing.". Mary said that normally she wouldn't have allowed so much TV viewing, but this was for educational purposes.

My vernacular was been improving. The time I spent watching *Let's Make a Deal*, *The Price is Right* and *Sesame Street* has been very advantageous toward my verbal development.

However, Mary did monitor what I was exposed too. She said that watching *All My Children* and *General Hospital* wouldn't help me understand family dynamics and the Healthcare industry.

I quite enjoyed "lounging" around all day in my soft, colorful pajamas. The antics of the big, yellow talking fowl and the green, dirty monster, living amongst the refuse, were extremely entertaining. However, my television privileges always came to an abrupt halt at noon, when lunch was served.

Roger would prepare his "authentic.", as he called it, fish and chips. For some reason I could not bring myself to consume the deep-fried, battered creatures. Roger always pretended not to be disappointed, but I knew he was hoping that just once, I'd attempt to enjoy his dish.

Not wanting to force me to do anything that would upset my stomach, Mary would make me homemade chicken soup. It was delicious.

After our meal Roger and I would clear the table and do the dishes. "We ain't got one of them energy sucking machines," Roger would repeat. "Since it's just Mary and me, we do things the old-fashioned way and wash 'em up in the sink." This was fine by me since I didn't know any other way to do dishes.

The afternoons were spent with Mary, Roger and me walking along the beach, not too close to the water per

Mary's request. Mary and Roger did all of the talking, of course. They told me about how they met, their schooling and various jobs and the history of Red Rock, the community they lived in.

Every word of their story was fascinating. They both had lived and were living very full lives. I just wished I could share the memories of my life experiences with them, but my mind would only recall painful imagines, and I still was unable to communicate verbally.

Before dinner I was allowed to choose one TV show to view. I chose *Little House on the Prairie*. I could tell it was a favorite of both Mary and Roger's.

"Classic," Roger would periodically say.

"Such a beautiful message," was Mary's frequent comment.

I enjoyed the show as well. Pa seemed the type of gentleman one would do well to model their deportment after, and that "half-pint" was an enjoyable character too.

Chapter 11
What's in a Name?

Dinner times were interesting to say the least. Each night Mary attempted to train me in the culinary arts. I was a dismal cook. My lasagna and spaghetti were always too salty and my shepherd's pie overcooked. The Starrs were very patient, and eventually I discovered I was good at cooking breakfast foods. So, for a few dinners we had French toast or scrambled eggs. I was happy I could contribute to providing us with nourishment.

Post dinner was my favorite time. After a warm bath with foamy bubbles, I changed into a clean pair of pajamas and nestled into my soft bed. Then Mary would read me to sleep. I think Roger thought her choice of reading material was a bit juvenile for me because Roger would often snicker and cover his mouth. I really enjoyed the stories of the little train that showed an amazing amount of tenacity, and the adventures of the boy, the bear and the dog were colorful and engaging.

Yes, my life had become quite predictable. However, I did enjoy the sense of stability. This morning though, I could tell something was going to be different.

Just as I placed a syrup covered piece of hot pancake in my mouth, Roger commandingly put his strong, rough hand on my shoulder and said, "It's settled. It's been long enough for someone to claim ya and nobody has." I listened with great anticipation.

"Well, we want ya. I mean if you'll have us, we'd like to be your family."

My heart felt like it was about to explode. I wanted to yell at the top of my lungs "Yes!" How could this family, who had known me for such a brief time, take me in as one of their own?

Roger stood and scratched his beard. "There is just something about you," he mumbled.

Mary closed her eyes and whispered, "A gift from the sea."

Roger took Mary's hands. "If he's gonna be part of the family we'll have to name 'em."

Mary swallowed hard and looked deep into Roger's eyes. They often exhibited the ability to communicate without having to speak, a gift I was envious of. Roger cleared his throat and spoke in a reverent tone. "We'd like to honor you with the name of Kyle." I smile and Roger continued softly. "You see, our son's name was Jeremy Kyle Starr."

Both Mary and Roger had wet eyes. I gave them the biggest grin of appreciation I could manufacture. The sides of my mouth even hurt a little. With respect I nodded my head emphatically. It was official, my new life had begun, my new life as a member of this wonderful family, my new life as Kyle Roger Starr.

Chapter 12
First Word

Mary and Roger sat on the sofa-couch with their mouths wide open. Mary put her hand over her lips and giggled. Roger gave her a stern look, "Stop it."

"That's it," Roger stood and folded his arms in front of him. "We are goin' to town!"

Mary could tell I didn't quite understand. "It's the clothes dear," Mary said pointing at my hand-picked outfit. "You need something that fits. Something, well something contemporary."

Mary explained I was running out of options. Roger had allowed me to wear some of his old clothes. Since Roger was what Mary referred to as, "the man of the house.", I wanted to look like him.

Apparently, Roger's oversized baggy plaid pants and bright yellow polo shirt weren't working for me. It was clothing he used to wear when he played a game called "golf.". It also didn't help that I had chosen to wear a bright blue cap from what Roger called his "younger and hipper days."

"It's time." Roger shook some shiny objects in his hands.

"Not in that old thing." Mary snatched the objects from Roger's hand. "You'll be taking mine."

Roger reluctantly accepted a new set of shiny objects from Mary.

"Come on," Roger commanded.

"Are you sure you are up for this honey?"

"Why wouldn't I be?" Roger replied.

Mary gently touched her heart. Roger waved off her gesture and summoned me to follow him. "Don't ya think Kyle would rather go shopping for clothes with his old man, and not his mommy?"

"Hmmm," was Mary's brief response.

Next thing I knew I was standing outside a large square structure. Roger wanted me to wait outside while he "started her up". I looked back at the lighthouse and smiled. I was thankful I had been taught the name of the cylinder that had brought me to the Starr family.

Beneath the lighthouse was our home. It was shorter than the lighthouse but still round. I had the suspicion that the Starr's home was unique and that other houses were not built to the same specifications.

BOOM!

I spun around and took a defensive posture. The fighting stance I had adopted was instinctive. I stared into the large open mouth of the box before me. It was too dark to see inside, but I was on guard for whatever might come forth.

A rattling sound filled the air and I stiffened. Two bright eyes shot out of the darkness. Alarmed, I jumped back and gritted my teeth.

Before I knew it, Roger had me inside a moving box. Even though it made a lot of noise and produced an enormous amount of smoke, I liked the bouncy seats. I laughed to myself thinking that now I was inside the terrifying monster I had been ready to do battle with.

The beast's exterior coat was a pleasant, faded blue color. The truck, as Roger called it, was fittingly named "Ol' Blue.".

Somehow I knew this was not the method of transportation Mary had meant for us to take. Roger said, "I always have a spare set of keys in the visor.". He was referencing the shiny objects Mary had previously confiscated.

Regardless of Mary's disdain for this mode of transportation, I was thrilled. The objects around me rushed by; trees, hills and lots of similar square shaped structures. "Houses," Roger explained. They looked very different from the round home Roger and Mary lived in.

As we approached the "city.", the houses grew bigger and taller. There was one very large house that groups of individuals, who looked like me, were going into. They were all shapes and sizes, wearing a variety of colorful and unique clothing.

We travelled for a few more minutes before stopping in front of a shiny building. The sign on the building read, *Teen Gear.*

"See those young chickadees strolling into the store?" Roger pointed at a group of very attractive girls. My eyes widened and I swallowed hard.

Roger began to chuckle. I realized I was nodding in time to the rapid beating of my heart. Roger gave me a gentle nudge with his elbow. My nodding ceased.

"Met your mom, I mean Mary, at a clothing outlet." Roger's smile grew as he became lost in his thoughts. I studied his face trying to ascertain what he was thinking.

"Here," Roger said, getting out of the car. "Let me show you how to be a gentleman."

Roger soon had me holding the store door open for what seemed like dozens of girls. Some smiled and others giggled, as they entered and exited the building.

Mary may not have been correct about Ol' Blue, but she was right on the mark when it came to my style of attire. From the looks I received, I knew that my appearance was the cause of their amusement.

"Time to get in," Roger insisted. "Can't stand out here forever."

As I stepped through the door I inadvertently bumped into a girl. The items she was carrying dropped to the ground. Some colorful footwear fell out of a box. Instinctively, I bent down to help her

When I handed her one of the boxes, our hands touched. I thought my heart had been racing before, now it was speeding and ready to explode. My eyes locked on a beautiful face, framed by silky, satin, soft flowing hair. I was drowning in her magnificent green eyes.

"Sorry Mr. Starr," she stood up.

"Are you alright dear?" Roger responded.

They knew each other! And now I wanted to know her.

"This is my nephew, Kyle."

The vision before me smiled and extended her hand. "Nice to meet you, Kyle. I'm-"

"Beautiful!" I exclaimed.

Chapter 13
Elvis Has Left the Building

"Amber!" I announced, bounding into the kitchen. "Amber the Beautiful!" I held my hand over my heart and sighed.

Stunned, Mary dropped the pot she was washing. The pot clanged on the floor and Mary stared at me, her mouth open. Roger walked in behind me and encouragingly slapped my back; this pushed me farther into the kitchen.

"Better close that pie hole, honey. You don't wanna go catching flies," Roger chuckled at his joke. I don't think Mary was amused, she just stared at me.

"Yep," Roger nonchalantly announced. "He can talk after all."

Mary took a seat at the kitchen table. "So I heard."

Roger picked up Mary's pot. "You drop this?" Mary snatched the pot from Roger and patted him on his behind. Roger feigned pain.

"Stop it," Mary chided.

"You love it," Roger winked at Mary. She smiled at him, paused, and shook her head.

"Wait. What else can he say?"

Roger shrugged his shoulders. "Lots of stuff." Roger raised his brows at me. "Right, Kyle!"

"Right Roger!" was my unbridled reply.

Mary put her hand over her mouth.

"Hello Mary." I extended my hand just as Amber had done.

Mary dispensed with the traditional-hand shake and embraced me. "Hello Kyle, hello."
I sure did love Mary's hugs.

I didn't know what felt better; my freedom of speech or the continuous pats on the back from Roger, accompanied by the reassuring hugs from Mary. The revelry came to a halt when Mary released me from her tender arms and took a step back.

"Two questions," Mary said looking me up and down. "What is Kyle wearing? And who is Amber?"

Roger snickered to himself. "You know, that sweet Amber Dawson, Major Dawson's daughter."

"And Kyle's clothing?"

Roger took a swig of soda from a bottle, avoiding having to give an immediate response.

"The King," I blurted out. "A little less conversation..."

Mary was speechless yet again.

The previous night on the small screen in the box, which Roger frequently would yell "stinkin' antenna" at as he hit it, there was a marvelous presentation for, "An Amazing Deal on Rock 'n Roll CD Box Sets. Wait and that's not all, we'll include this commemorative plate."

The commercial was about a man name Elvis Presley, The King of Rock 'n Roll. For some reason the word "King" struck a chord with me, so I decided if it was good enough for the "King,", it was good enough for me. And to be a King, you needed to dress like one.

Obviously Mary did not approve of my sequined white jumpsuit and red neckerchief.

"I am having a hard time believing that getup came from a store where the kids shop," Mary protested.

I looked to Roger for assistance. Roger chuckled. "Sure didn't."

"Then where?" Mary persisted.

"Those prices are outrageous!" I said, trying my best to imitate Roger's voice. Roger took another swig of his soda. "We went to the Thrifty Mart."

"No!" Mary was aghast.

"Sure did," I said grinning. Roger couldn't help snickering. "After ol' blue eyes run in with Miss Amber, I thought it be best to take him some place less populated with the "beauties"."

Roger twitched two fingers on both his hands as he said the word "beauties.". I assumed this was to emphasize the word referring to all those pretty girls, especially Amber.

"Beauties," I mused. "Beauty with the green eyes."

Imagining Amber's captivating eyes, brought another Elvis song out of me, "Love me tender, love me true."

Even Mary was laughed this time.

"Who needs a radio?" Roger nudged Mary, causing her to continue laughing.

"Alright, alright." Mary raised her hands up. "Please fetch me my measuring tape, dear."

"You're not gonna make the boy clothes!"

"It's in my sewing kit."

Roger sighed and put his soda down. Reluctantly he went into the next room. I sensed impending doom.

"Oh Kyle," Mary said putting her arm around me. "You better go change."

I frowned at the thought of having to relinquish my outfit.

"Go on, Elvis," said Mary. "We can always resurrect it for Halloween."

As I left for my room I gave Mary one last parting gesture so she'd know I wasn't upset with her request. With a signature Elvis shake of my hips I sang out, "Well, that's all right, little mama." Then I rounded the corner and headed to my room.

Mary put her hand in front of her mouth and giggled. From that moment on, "little mama" was a tender nickname I would often call her.

Chapter 14
Curious Kyle

The power of speech was a wonderful gift. I had some many questions to ask and so much appreciation I needed to express. Mary said I had become quite loquacious.

I liked Mary's command of the English language. She had a wonderful vocabulary. Roger too, just in a more everyday verbiage.

For the next few days I continued to thank Mary and Roger for their gracious hospitality. Roger would chuckle when Mary would remind me that I had already thanked them enough, and that it was all right if I didn't continue to say "thank you", over and over again. I couldn't help myself, I was just so, so, so grateful.

Between my words of gratitude, I asked Mary and Roger to tell me the names of various household items and appliances. I loved gathering this information. We went from room to room, and I soaked it all in like a sponge.

"What's that?" I'd inquire, followed with, "And what's it used for?"

It was a live version of the Discovery Channel, except the TV didn't sigh when I forgot a name of an item, followed by me asking its place of origin, and if Mary and Roger would be kind enough to use it in a sentence. I learned that one from a film called Spellbound. Mary had shown me that piece of cinematic genius one rainy day, and I must say I was captivated. This was of course before I had the gift of speech.

At least it was a gift to me. I hoped that Mary and Roger felt so too, and that my incessant inquiries weren't becoming overbearing to them. But I could not help myself, I was so happy and excited to finally be able to communicate.

In the middle of touring the house, Roger announced, "Let's mix things up a little shall we."

Roger took me to the garage. What I once referred to as the monster's cave, became a treasure trove of wonders. A plethora of tools and gadgets covered the garage walls and tables.

The only drawback to my freedom of speech was my lack of memory. Roger and Mary asked questions of me too, but I couldn't give them the real answers they were looking for. I told them everything that I could remember, which wasn't much. I even shared with them my visions or nightmares.

Mary was perplexed and couldn't make sense of my accounts. Roger however was very intrigued. "We'll get to the bottom of this," he said. "Don't you worry."

I wasn't, I was happy and content.

Now that I could audibly communicate, Mary said it was time to make the necessary preparation that would allow for my entering into a place where I could expand my social interactions and increase my intellect. A magical place called High School.

Chapter 15
Social Studies

Mary had decided it was time to introduce me the world of "online shopping.". She and I sat at her computer table.

"This will help me look like a High School student?"

"Just you wait," Mary said.

Mary pressed a few buttons and the screen lit up. Color images of all types of clothing flashed before my eyes.

So many choices; it was very exciting and a bit overwhelming. I was fascinated with the instantaneous pictures that appeared on command. Mary's fingers flew over the little rectangles that were covered in individual letters. She told me it was the alphabet, just not in proper order.

Roger periodically came up behind me to check the scar on the side of my head.

"Musta got conked pretty hard to cause all this amnesia.", he repeatedly say

"Well, Mary will learn ya good." Was Roger closing remark, until next visit.

It didn't feel like relearning to me. I really believed that I had never seen or heard of some of the things that I was now being introduced to. Somehow, somewhere deep inside me I knew I was not indigenous to the world I was now a part of. But I so desperately wanted to be, thus the need to procure suitable clothing.

Roger and Mary had varied opinions, as to what the teens are wearing today. Fortunately I was given the final say when it came to the order. Once my selections had been made, Mary explained that it would take several days for my purchases to arrive.

Several days? How could people be expected to wait so long for such wonderful gifts from cyberspace? Roger was amused at my anxiety and ignorance about the workings of the computer. He said we had a lot in common.

In the meantime, Roger committed to instruct me in the ways of "wooing.". It will be one thing to look the part, but to act the part is a whole different kettle of fish.

Roger's lessons in the arena of social skills consisted of long walks along the beach, where he would proudly tell me stories of his glory days in High School, and what it took to finally win Mary's heart. The other portion of my education came from some of Roger and Mary's favorite old movies. They explained that chivalry was a dying art and proper etiquette would make friends, influence people, and win a maiden's heart.

I enjoyed our conversations and watching their selections of films. The non-colorful ones where the characters moved their mouths, but no voices could be heard reminded me of my first days with the Starrs. Now that I could speak Mary insisted in enhancing my social studies as well. She introduced me to the wonderful realm of BOOKS!

Chapter 16
Readers are Leaders

Books were amazing! The knowledge they contained was endless and reading just for "pleasure and leisure.", as Mary called it, was equally enjoyable. Roger said I could find the same "stuff" on the internet, but there was something almost magical about turning the pages of an encyclopedia or fiction novel. I devoured book after book. I couldn't put them down.

Non-fiction and fiction books were phenomenal, and then there was poetry. Mary said a good dose of Emerson, Dickinson and Angelou would do wonders for the mind.

When I asked Roger and Mary if they thought I was spending too much time reading, Roger handed me one of his favorite books called, Gifted Hands. It was about an amazing young man who eventually became a world-renowned doctor, and it all started with his momma requiring him to read and write reports on books.

Mary was convinced that if I kept up my reading and learning that I too would become someone of influence.

Day after day I read. The books helped me stay calm while waiting for my impending packages to arrive.

One afternoon it finally happened. I was with Roger, having our daily walk and talk on the beach, and Mary called for me to come to the house. She waved two tan colored parcels in the air.

"They've arrived!" I shouted. I turned to Roger for his approval.

"Go get 'em son."

"Thank you sir," I replied. The etiquette lessons were paying off. I pressed the book I had been reading into Roger's chest. He laughed. It was a copy of *The Miraculous Journey of Edward Tulane*, a story about a special, yet artificial, bunny's adventures and his self-discovery.

Roger didn't mind me reading books during our conversations. He said at times it was much the same way with Mary; she being the avid reader she was.

I shook Roger's available hand and sprinted toward the house. Roger cheered me on. "Faster Kyle, faster."

I picked up my speed. Even the heavy rubber boots I was wearing weren't going to slow me down. I didn't even pause for the flock of seagulls that were several feet in front of me. They had landed early to consume the remains of Roger's over-barbecued hotdog and bun.

"Fly! Be free!" I yelled as I ran straight through the middle of the flock. The birds scattered every which way.

Within seconds I was beside Mary on the grass. "Phew, you're a quick one," she said. "Are you sure you want to open these now, Kyle?" Mary put the packages behind her back. I gulped with confusion. Mary's tender smile eliminated all doubts. She obviously was aware of my anxiousness and was playfully teasing me.

I gained composure and gave a gentleman's bow. "My lady," I said. "It would give me great pleasure if you would allow me the honor of opening those prized boxes immediately, if not sooner."

Mary couldn't help herself and I received one of her cherished hugs. "What has my sweetheart been teaching you?"

I grinned and graciously accepting the packages from Mary.

"Go on." She gave me a light pat on the bottom. I feigned pain, just as I'd seen Roger do, and then raced to the house.

"Thanks, little momma," I yelled over my shoulder.

Chapter 17
Over Indulgence

Tada! I rejoiced, greeting Roger and Mary, the moment they stepped through the front door.

I was dressed up in the latest teen attire; a pair of jeans, a hoodie and some footwear with a little jumping man on them. Everything fit perfectly! Now I was really beginning to feel a part of this world, and tomorrow I was going to enter the magical world of High School.

"School is not just for fish", Roger explained. "School of Fish" was also the name of an alternative rock band that had a brief run in the early 90s. This was according to Roger, who claimed to be a "trivia king.". This self-proclaimed title must have been amusing because when Roger mentioned it, Mary always put her hand over her mouth and tried to camouflage a giggle.

Now looked the part, Roger provided me with one final instructional film.

"Now watch the way Gene Kelly makes these women swoon," insisted Roger as he sat beside me on the couch. He kept offering me his mixture of popcorn, chocolate covered peanuts, and BBQ chips.

"One caveat," interjected Mary, from the kitchen. "Hold back on the tap dancing."

Roger leaned over and whispered to me, "If you feel the rhythm, you let loose, kid."

"I heard that," Mary said, stepping into the room. She had been lovingly preparing a school lunch for me to take tomorrow.

Roger hopped to his feet and took Mary in his arms.

"Don't try and tell me that's not what won you over." Mary giggled as Roger waltzed her around the room.

"You best learn a step or two yourself, Kyle," Roger admonished. "Them school hops are great for meeting young ladies."

Watching Roger and Mary turn and spin, caused me to smile. My amusement was short lived, and my smile was replaced by a frown. Mary took notice.

"Are you okay, Kyle?"

"Don't be jealous," joked Roger. "You'll get your turn, dancing with Mary of course." Roger chuckled at his own joke.

I wanted to laugh at Roger's humor, I really did. However, what was happening in my stomach was no joke. My belly began making unusual sounds.

"Kyle!" Mary's eyes widened. "You're as white as a sheet."

Mary and Roger stopped dancing and looked at me with great concern.

"This can't be good," Roger said sheepishly. "I know that look all too well."

Mary scowled at Roger. "What did you feed our boy?!"

Before Roger could answer, I made a noise that sounded like a cross between the lion I had seen at the beginning of Mary's movies and an explosion of dynamite. Something was coming out, and coming out fast.

All of the treats Roger had encouraged me to consume wanted to leave my body. I frantically searched for the nearest container.

The half-eaten bowl of popcorn was the closest in proximity. After a horrific noise and a terrified look from both Mary and Roger, the recent contents of my stomach were expelled into the once cherished bowl.

Chapter 18
Nervous Night

Mary tucked me into bed and placed a wet cloth on my forehead

"In the future, you may wish to avoid over indulging in combination of all those treats."

"I'm sorry little mama."

"You don't have to apologize, Kyle. I'm not mad."

"Not Roger either, right?"

Mary winked and kissed my forehead goodnight and opened my window, allowing the fresh evening air to permeate my room. While Mary's back was turned, Roger poked his head in my room. He gave me a quick smile and nod before Mary could turn around and discover him.

Perhaps my overindulgence with Roger's concoctions wasn't the only cause of my nausea. I guess I was a bit nervous about attending school, but the movie treats exacerbated the situation.

Mary was right; the night air coupled with the sound of the crashing waves helped me drift off to the land of slumber.

Dreams are fascinating; whether caused by subconscious thoughts or insufficiently digested food, like my gluttony of treats, they produce vivid movies of the mind.

Images of the dream are thought to originate in the visual center of the cerebral cortex, the brain's grey matter and the mind's hub for memory, awareness, consciousness, and thought. Yes, Mary had a good book on the study of dreams.

My dream had a pleasant enough beginning, very pleasant actually. My mind had replaced Mr. Kelly, in a scene from the movie where he dances with a little gray mouse, with me. I wasn't exultant about wearing the sailor suit, but when the mouse transformed into a cartoon version of Amber, I forgot about the ridiculous outfit.

Cartoon Amber and I danced around the same movie set room, but we were quickly transitioned to frolicking on top of the ocean. This was highly unusual and amusing. The water was our dance floor, solid and smooth. We glided across it like Fred and Ginger. Yes, I was exposed to the best of the musical productions, courtesy of both Roger and Mary.

My mind was not able to distinguish between the real world and the dream world. It was such a visceral experience. I could really feel Amber's hands in mine, tangible and warm, even though she was in animated form. It was funny, but as I smiled in the dream, I knew I was really smiling, as I lay on my soft bed, in the comfort and safety of the Starr's home.

I tried hard to control my dream and transform Amber into her lovely human form, but the harder I tried the darker the scene became. The music came to an abrupt stop and our dancing ended just as suddenly as it began.

I stood frozen in fear, on top of the solid water floor. Amber was being pulled away from me.

"No Amber! Please stay with me!" The words were loud in my mind, but not a sound came out of my wide, open mouth. A single tear formed at the corner of Amber eye, and slowly traveled down her cheek. In desperation I reached for her.

My hands! Fish-like scales covered them and the webbing between my fingers was back. Amber shrieked. Now I could hear her voice, loud and frightened.

I looked at my hands in horror, the same horror I felt the night I washed up on the beach. I touched my face and it felt scaly too. The reflection in the glass sea below me revealed a boy covered in scales, with bulging eyes and sea green hair.

The dream was now, undeniably a nightmare.

Chapter 19
Sinking Feeling

No! I looked back at Amber and the floor beneath her liquefied. She slowly sank into the dark water.

I attempted to race toward her, but I was too late. After slipping several times on the watery floor, I reached Amber's position just as she sank out of sight.

I shrieked, and this time I could hear myself. My agonizing screech was so loud and powerful that the floor beneath me cracked and spread apart. It reminded me of a cartoon I had inadvertently watched about a little penguin in the middle of the ocean. He was frantically hopping from one piece of breaking ice to another, attempting to stay afloat. I had smiled at the penguin's antics then, but now I wasn't grinning.

I wasn't able to jump from the broken pieces of the floor like the penguin had done with the ice, and I soon found myself floating alone in endless water.

Everywhere I looked was water, and nothing else. The water was cold, very cold. My teeth chattered and I shivered violently. My shaking almost woke me up.

I wish it had, because before I knew it I was surrounded by a frenzy of sharks. I closed my eyes and wished I was awake in the real world. When I opened my eyes, I was submerged in the water and the sharks were within a few feet of me. All of them were baring their teeth. Strange, it was as if they were smiling at me, not in a narcissistic way, but more of a display of admiration.

The terrible fish lost their grins and fear filled their once expressionless eyes. I turned my head from side to side, looking for the cause of their alarm. I saw nothing. There was nothing for them to fear, nothing but me. Then I saw myself with a sinister grin and bloodshot eyes. The sharks quickly turned to swim away, but there was no escape for them. I attacked them with fury

What was I doing? I was out of control, ravenous and destructive. Before the scene became too graphic I bolted upright in bed.

I was covered in perspiration. My train pajamas were soaked. I paused for a moment, leaned over my bed, and promptly threw up.

Chapter 20
Back to Reality

During breakfast I kept apologizing to Mary for the deposit I had made on the bedroom floor. Mary asked me to refrain from such talk at the table. Roger reassured me that with a little elbow grease the stain on my carpet would come out. I wondered how the human body could produce such an abundance of fluids.

"You never cease to crack me up son," Roger chuckled.

"Sorry for my ignorance."

"Nonsense," Mary said. "Just finish your toast dear."

I looked longingly at the scrambled eggs on Mary and Roger's plate. "Better stick with bread champ." Roger made a choking jester, and pretended to stick his finger down his throat. Mary playfully slapped his hand.

"Stop that."

"Oooops!" Roger put a fork full of egg in his mouth and raised his eyebrows at me.

I couldn't help smiling. My "tummy", as Mary called it, was feeling on the mend, but I had to agree with Mary, I better not chance it.

"You excited Kyle?" Roger asked.

"Yes sir."

Mary gently touched my shoulder. "Perhaps a tiny bit nervous too?"

I nodded sheepishly.

"No shame in that Kyle," Mary continued. "New experiences and people often cause butterflies."

I scrunched my face up. "I am somewhat apprehensive; however, I have not seen any butterflies this morning."

Roger laughed so hard that some coveted pieces of egg flew from his mouth. Mary just shook her head. She wasn't amused with Roger's insensitivity. The "you know better" lecture was certain to be given to Roger once I was away from the house.

"I do see seagulls though!" I enthusiastically exclaimed pointing out the window.

This time Roger's laughter caused him to choke and he motioned to Mary for his freshly squeezed orange juice.

"Serves you right," Mary said as she handed it over.

"We need to get you a stand-up gig at Chuckles," Roger said, gulping down his orange juice.

Roger went on to explain that Chuckles was a local café and comedy spot. Apparently, Roger had been a big hit there in his day. Was there anything Roger wasn't good at? I really admired him, especially the way he was able to charm his way out of trouble with Mary. I hoped to grow up to be a man like Roger.

Watching them interacting at breakfast caused me to reflect on the weeks that had passed since I had been discovered on the beach. My feelings for this wonderful couple had grown deep and strong. I was very fortunate to be part of their life and honored to be a member of their family. I resolved to represent the family well during the new adventure I was about to embark on.

Chapter 21
The Big Day

After Mary's delicious toast breakfast, and a few more social skill lessons from Roger; including refraining from overusing the word "beautiful", I was dressed and ready for High School.

Roger wanted to have me walk the ½ mile down the lane to what he called the "pick up point." There I would take the big yellow tube that transported the sometimes not so enthusiastic students to school.

Mary thought it best, at least for my first day, that she took me to school.

We sang show tunes during our drive. Well, Mary sang, I really didn't know the words, so I attempted to hum along.

"Do you want me to walk in with you?" Mary inquired.

"Sure, Little Mama!" I enthusiastically responded.

I did not realize teenage boys were not supposed to be escorted to school by their "mommies

"Hi.", "Hello.", "How are you?" I couldn't help smiling while greeting my fellow students. I strutted through the hallways of my new school, making eye contact with everyone I could. Roger would have been proud.

Mary was smiling too, but I think it was out of amusement. Some passersby smiled back, but the majority shook their head at me and glared.

Soon, we met the principal. Mary explained that principal was his title and not his first name. His first name was Hank, but I was only to refer to him using his title and last name.

"Thank you for allowing me to attend your prestigious school Principal Stern." I said, shaking Hank's, I mean Principle Stern's hand.

"I don't know if you'd call Red Rock High prestigious, but you're welcome." Principal Stern turned to Mary.

"He seems like a bright enough boy."

"Oh, he is!" Mary answered proudly. "And he loves reading, pretty much anything he can get his hands on."

"Hmmm," Principal Stern grunted. "As long as he keeps in line."

He looked me straight in the eyes, through his small rimmed glasses. "We didn't establish rules just for the fun of it. Rules are for the betterment of the students."

I gulped and looked at Mary. She gave me a warm smile. It made me feel everything was going to be all right.

Principal Stern sat down behind his desk.

"All your paperwork seems to be in order. I suppose you are officially a Rooster now."

"Who?" I said.

Mary put her hand on my shoulder. "It is the school name, dear, The Red Rock Roosters."

Interesting how the schools were named after barnyard animals, or jungle animals, or even insects.

"So, nephew, eh?"

"Yes," replied Mary. "On Roger's side, of course."

Principal Stern sat up straight. "Oh, I see." He then gave me another look over and nodded. Standing up, he extended his hand. I shook it emphatically. "Welcome to Red Rock High School Mr. Starr."

While we walked back through the hallway, Mary explained that Hank and Roger had played football together in High School. "Nothing bonds a couple of fellas like chasing the pigskin through the mud," Mary told me.

I enjoyed how Mary's vernacular changed when she spoke about Roger. She would use his terminology as a form of admiration for her husband. Roger knew it too, since he said Mary was a clever gal, too clever for him, being a former "Educator" and all.

I smiled at Mary, and once again thought about the love she and Roger had for each other. I wondered if I had ever loved someone like that. Of course, I couldn't remember, and I had no internal emotions to validate such a thought, but there was always room for hope.

If I hadn't ever loved anyone so completely, maybe I could learn. My mind immediately thought of the beautiful Amber. I crossed my fingers and hoped our paths would connect again, and soon.

"In all my years," Mary said, "I don't think I've seen anyone so elated to be starting High School."

I hugged Mary. "Thank you, thank you Mary; for all that you have given me."

"This is your lunch money." Mary grinned and handed me some of those green papers with the pictures of the elderly gentlemen on them, the same kind that Roger had used to procure my Elvis outfit.

"Thanks!" I was very excited to see what I could accumulate with these paper marked with the numeral one.

I gave Mary another hug. Students walked by and snickered. Mary and I said our goodbyes, and I was off in time to find my first class.

Chapter 22
First Friend

The bell rang, and the hallway instantly flooded with students. It was going to be nearly impossible to greet all these new colleagues. Thankfully, I received a light tap on my shoulder. I turned around to discover a boy, just a little shorter than myself.

"I'm Ian," he said, pushing up his black rimmed glasses.

"Hi!" I shouted "Pleased to meet you, I am Kyle Roger Starr."

"Whoa," Ian chuckled. "You must be new, such enthusiasm."

"I am new Ian, very new."

"Where are you headed Kyle Roger Starr?"

I held up my list of assigned classes. "This is my first destination Ian."

"No way! Algebra with Mr. Mon!" Now Ian was shouting. "That's my class too."

"Way!" I said.

Ian laughed, and his glasses slid down his nose. Pushing them up again, Ian said, "This way my man, just follow the yellow brick road."

There was no road made of yellow bricks for us to travel on, and I soon came to discover that Ian loved using movie references every chance he could, but usually they were slightly out of context.

"We've arrived!" Ian held the class room door open for me. "You can sit by me."

"Thanks, Ian."

We sat in the very front row. Ian assured me that geniuses sat in the front row.

"Is that Mr. Mon?" I inquired, pointing to a very large male who had just walked into the room.

"No," laughed Ian. "That's Ant-Man."

I tilled my head and scrunched my face. I was confused. I have recently viewed an animated show about a struggling colony of ants. The gentleman Ian was referring to didn't have any visible insect characteristics. In fact, this male was quite large.

"You know, from the comics?"

Comics? Most of my reading was about History, Geography and Science. Roger did sneak the occasional Young Adult Romance novel in for me to read. He said it might help me understand how the young chickadees think, but if Mary asked then I was supposed to say that the book didn't come from him. These comics sounded intriguing though.

Ian continued, "The hero that was as small as a bug and then became a giant?"

"Fascinating." I rapidly nodded. "I have not come across this documentation in my studies."

Ian stared at me with a blank expression for a few moments, then shook his head.

"Yeah, Tommy was shorter than me last year and then over the summer, boom!" Ian clapped his hands together. "Now he is the Center for the Roosters."

"Wow!" My mouth dropped open.

"I know, pretty amazing right." Ian leaned back in his chair, and put his hands behind his head. "My day will come though, I'm Batman."

Ian's somewhat protruding teeth, and small rounded ears did give him a certain rodent like appearance, but I would have said more mouse than bat.

However, my "Wow" utterance was not in response to Ian's tall tale. *She*… had just walked into the room.

Amazing, crossing your fingers really did work.

The pounding of my heart muffled Ian's words as he continued to pontificate about the vital importance of reading and studying comic books.

Noticing my daze, Ian waved his hand in front of my face. Blinking, I refocused on Ian's closing words to his lengthy monologue. "Not a chance on earth," he said. "You might as well be from Krypton."

Chapter 23
School Rules

Ian's explanation of the Superman reference was confusing. He said that Superman, aka Clark Kent, loved Lois Lane and that she loved him, and it was their love that allowed them to be together against all odds.

"Ha, ha," Ian covered his mouth to avoid drawing too much attention. "It's just a saying, my saying. I wasn't inferring that you and Amber, in any way, shape or form, resemble the Man of Steel and his lovely ace reporter."

I gulped with embarrassment. My interest in Amber was apparently very obvious. Ian said it was my flushed red face, and "Cheshire Cat" smile that gave me away.

I couldn't help myself, especially when she actually acknowledged me with a smile and wave. Not just any smile, but a perfectly formed smile, and an ever-so-friendly wave. At least I assumed she was directing her gestures at me.

Peering over my shoulder, I didn't see anyone behind me responding, so her greeting was definitely intended for me. A warm, blissful feeling of happiness filled me;

the same feeling I had during our first awkward encounter.

Amber took her seat.

"Come back down to earth and quit gawking," Ian said.

"Do you want to get yourself killed?"

"Why would I want that?" I replied.

"Dudes like us can't be making nice with girls like Amber Louise Dawson."

My face lit up once again as new information was provided about this enchanting girl.

"No," Ian demanded. "Now wipe that infatuated grin off your face."

I literally took my hand and wiped my mouth. Ian laughed out loud.

"Ha, you're a funny dude."

"Oh. Thank you, Ian." I assumed this was a compliment.

"Hey, I don't mean to discourage your romantic inclinations, but..."

Ian halted. I expected another piece of wise, friendly advice, but Ian stared straight ahead at the door. His mouth seemed to be forming some words, but nothing was coming out.

"Ian? Are you okay?"

"Code Red!" Ian motioned for me to glance in the direction of Ian's hypnotic gaze.

Framed in the doorway was a very attractive girl in a brown, red and white uniform with a picture of a rooster on the back that matched other girls, who were already seated in the room. Across the front of their uniforms was the school name, RED ROCK.

Immediately behind the girl was an extremely large boy. He was so big that he filled the entire door frame.

Ian's eyes were still fixed on the door. What could have caused his use of another famous movie line? Was it the attractive female, or the huge hulking figure behind her?

As the couple walked down our row, Ian ducked his head and whispered, "That's my Lois Lane."

"Wouldn't he be Superman then?" I whispered back.

"No!" Ian's retort was sharp. "He's Bizzaro, if anyone."

"Huh," I mused for a moment. "Why don't you ask your soul mate out to the malt shop?"

Ian stared at me with indignant eyes.

"What?"

"That is how Roger wooed Mary."

"Who did what?" Ian shook his head. "Where are you from?"

"The Lighthouse," I cheerfully responded.

"Ha!" Ian patted me on the shoulder. "Well listen, Mr. Lighthouse."

Leaning toward Ian, I waited for more words of impending wisdom.

Chapter 24
Ian's Instruction

Ian surveyed the room. He nodded and motioned for me to come closer.

"There are a few things you gotta know."

"Yes?" I said, picking up my pen.

"Good idea. Jot this down." Ian cleared his throat. "Number one. Guys like us, don't go after girls like those."

Ian subtly pointed toward Amber and his "Lois Lane".

"Guys like us?"

"Yeah, you know... the nerdy, genius types."

"We're the Peter Parkers of the school, nerdy yet super smart, but not much for athletics. With the sports thing we're more like Plastic Man."

Interesting how Ian put me in this category with him, considering we had just become acquaintances. I began to take notes, but Ian was spewing forth wisdom too fast for me to keep up. So, I put my pen down and listened intently.

"Number two. We always eat lunch at a designated table. I will reveal it to you later, once you have taken the oath that is."

"Oath?"

"Yeah, now stay with me."

Ian leaned in and talked in a low voice.

"Third, and probably the most important. If you want to survive here, you must..."

An energetic man bounced into the classroom wearing dark glasses, and a very, very bright, multicolored shirt.

"Hey, Mr. Mon!" Ian blurted out.

"Hey, yourself young Padawan."

Ian smiled with delight. He was not ashamed, or reserved about showing his admiration toward this gentleman.

"It's him," Ian said proudly. "The Teacher."

"Oh?"

"Mr. Mon is the Man!" Ian exclaimed, loud enough for our classmates to look over and snicker. Ian didn't seem to be affected though.

Mr. Mon sat on the edge of his desk. "Welcome to another fun filled day of learning! You are fortunate enough to begin your day with me. Wise choice I must say."

Ian raised his hand, and looked over at me. Mr. Mon mirrored Ian and raised his hand. "Your Jedi mind trick is working Ian." The class chuckled. "I shall now grant your request."

Grabbing some official looking papers off his desk Mr. Mon stood up.

"Students, we have the distinguished pleasure of having a bright new face amongst us." Gesturing to me Mr. Mon continued, "Kyle Starr, please rise and come forward."

My stomach rumbled as I stood up. *"Please no,"* I began having that feeling from the night I polluted my body with Roger's junk food. I looked down at Ian.

"May the force be with you," he whispered.

Facing a room full of my fellow students, I stood speechless, frozen with fear.

Chapter 25
Bully Zone

There were so many rules, both at home and at school. I was about to learn another rule of life, the strong prey on the perceived weak.

Beads of perspiration formed on my forehead and my arm pits felt moist. I surveyed the room and found the kindest eyes looking back at me. Her soft smile and encouraging nod saved me. My stomach settled, and my mind cleared.

"My name is Kyle, Kyle Roger Starr." I smiled brightly. "I live in the Lighthouse."

Giggles and chuckles permeated throughout the classroom.

"Kyle lives with Roger and Mary Starr, the Lighthouse keepers." Mr. Mon came to my rescue. "They are Kyle's aunt and uncle, and now his legal guardians," Mr. Mon paused, and his demeanor became serious, "due to the tragic loss of his parents."

The classroom became awkwardly silent.

Prior to attending my first day of school, Roger and Mary had sat me down and explained the art of equivocation. They were not going to have to lie to the school about my origin, because I was really lost from whatever parents I did have. Roger and Mary were my new protectors; thus, they were guarding me. Legal, was the word Mr. Mon chose to use.

No one questioned why Roger and Mary had darker skin than I did. Ian said it was cool and went on to explain that he was from a blended background too, like Dean Cain.

"Who?"

"Sup from Lois and Clark," Ian shook his head. "I know, I know, before our time, but my mom is still a huge fan. I am more of a Smallville supporter myself, but hey, The Man of Steel is The Man of Steel."

Now I was more determined than ever to procure some of these highly acclaimed comic books Ian loved so dearly. I hoped that becoming familiar with the superhero vernacular would strengthen the bonds of friendship Ian and I were forming.

After a barrage of introductions in every new class, I was ready to pack up for the day. While turning the combination on my locker, I felt a hand gently press on my shoulder. My whole body shivered with delight.

Chapter 26
Beauty's Beast

Without having to turn around, I knew the soft touch came from Amber. I took a deep breath and faced her. Wow, those green eyes were stunning and mesmerizing. I forgot to let my breath out. Amber's beautiful eyes widened with concern.

"Your face," she said. "It's turning blue."

I quickly exhaled and dizzily fell back into my locker.

"Are you okay?" Amber said, holding onto me.

"Oh, thanks. I probably just need some food."

Really, I wanted to let Amber know that her mere presence was intoxicating, and her genuine concern for my wellbeing made my heart swell with joy.

Before I could utter any words close to those, Amber pulled what she called a nutrition bar from her backpack.

"It's supposed to be healthy, but it actually tastes good too."

"Thank you, thank you so much. You are ever so kind."

Amber brushed her hair from the side of her face. "I just wanted to tell you I was sorry to hear about your parents. I lost my mom three years ago."

I knew that Amber's use of the word lost had the deep and tragic meaning Mary had once explained to me.

"Thank you, and I am sorry about your mom."

Amber looked at the floor for a moment and then gave me a small smile. "You're very polite, and you say thank you a lot."

"Oh, thank you for the compliment." The words came out before I could even think.

Amber giggled softly. "Well, I better get to practice. Good talking with you Kyle."

"Thank.... I mean, good talking with you too, Amber." I really enjoyed saying her name.

As I watched her walk down the hallway, I felt my tummy rumble. I studied the health bar she had graciously given me. Maybe I should eat her gift now. No, I would hold onto it for a little while longer.

Bam! My head slammed into my locker. My legs went numb and I slid down my locker, only to be held up by a fist grabbing my shirt.

"Watch what you are gawking at, lighthouse boy!"

Blinking my eyes cleared my blurred vision and I saw a young man, holding me up by my shirt with his clenched fist. He was wearing one of the school uniform jackets. It had a patch on it, of an oblong shaped ball.

"Give me that!" The jacket wearing attacker violently snatched my prize possession.

"Take it easy, Brad," a deep voice, and even larger boy said.

Brad, who must have been in one of my classes, since he knew my story, snapped back at the larger fellow, "I got this, Big Mike!"

Brad held up the nutrition bar. "I don't give her these things so she can pawn 'em off on some loser."

I looked down at my empty hand and back up at Brad. *Why he deprived me of Amber's gift, and in such a violent manner?*

A couple more boys with school jackets arrived on the scene. "Dudes, we better split, Stern is making the rounds."

"Stay away from my girl!" With one last shove into my locker, Brad and his boys were off.

My heart felt like it had just cracked. The one known as Big Mike, put his hand on my shoulder, and fear struck me. His touch was nowhere near as compassionate as Amber's.

"Take it easy, kid."

I held my breath and nodded. Once Big Mike walked away, I slid down the front of my locker and slumped on the floor. Of course, the most gorgeous girl in school would be connected to a boy like that. What was I thinking? I'd seen enough TV teen dramas to know better.

Beads of sweat formed on my forehead and I shook.

SNAP! FIZZ! The two sounds pulled me out of my comatose state. Ian stood above me with his hand stretched out. He was holding a colorful can that was producing fizzing noises and tiny bubbles.

"Figured you could use one." Ian smiled and handed me a colorful aluminum can.

Chapter 27
School Blues

But I don't want to go to school!" I protested, pulling the warm bed covers back over my head.

Mary stood by my bedside with a steaming plate of her famous scrambled eggs. The smell was intoxicating, my stomach growled, and the inside of my mouth became very moist. Okay, she won. I would eat, but no school.

Before I knew it, I was sitting at the kitchen table in my "rocket ship" print PJs. Mary placed two pieces of fresh toast next to my half-eaten plate of eggs. "Best you eat it up. You'll be doing a lot of walking today."

Roger stood at the counter, making his fresh-squeezed orange juice. He would not allow store bought OJ in this house. Roger chuckled at Mary's comment.

"What? Walk?" I said with a mouth full of toast and egg.

Mary handed me a napkin to wipe the corner of my mouth. "Kyle, it's not polite to speak with a mouth full of food."

I gulped the food down hard. "Pardon me little mama."

"Here is your permission slip Kyle," Mary said, sliding a yellow piece of paper across the table to me. I picked it up and read the words, "Aquarium Science Trip."

"Aquarium?"

"Yeah, it's like a zoo for fish." Roger squeezed a last drop of juice from his orange.

I knew what an aquarium was; I had seen a show about it on the PBS channel; the station of choice whenever Mary had control of the remote.

"But I don't want to go to school," I said sheepishly before taking another bite of food.

Moving her chair next to mine, Mary gave me a warm hug. "I know your first day was rough, but please trust me, it will get better."

"She ain't the only fish in the sea kid," Roger said sipping his homemade OJ. "Oh, you gotta try this."

Last night, I told Mary and Roger all about my day. They were empathetic and validated my feelings, which seemed to help, however I still felt a pinch of pain in my heart.

"Besides, what would little what's his name do without his new buddy?"

"His name is Ian dear," Mary told Roger.

"I guess I shouldn't quit after one day," I confessed.

Mary clapped her hands with delight, and Roger raised his glass. "That's the spirit, kid. Go get em."

"Thanks." I hugged Mary. She was so encouraging.

"Now go get changed, and brush your teeth. We'll get you to the bus on time."

I put my plate in the sink and Roger handed me a fresh glass of juice. "Better drink this up before brushing your teeth. It don't taste so great right after."

"Thank you," I said swallowing the juice. Roger was right; this was "dang" good juice.

Chapter 28
Bus Buddies

We arrived at school just, as a big yellow bus was pulling out of the parking lot. Roger was able to flag the driver down. The driver opened the doors and Roger put his foot on the bottom step.

"Got room for one more, Earl?"

"You joining us today, Starr?" The driver chuckled.

Roger pulled me from around the corner. "My Kyle needs to join his class."

"Well, hop aboard Kyle," Earl cheerful invited. "The more the merrier."

Roger and Earl shook hands. "Thanks pal."

"Tell Mary hello for me."

"You bet, and give Caroline our best."

With that the doors closed. The bonds of friendship seemed to cause people to act with kindness. Speaking of friendship, there was Ian, bouncing up and down on his seat, motioning for me to join him. His behavior made me glad I had found such a friend.

"Kyle, Kyle, over here." Ian's enthusiasm caused laughter from the back of the bus, but today, I didn't care.

"Hi, Ian!"

"So glad you made it Kyle, this place is the bomb."

Ian's colorful terms were always amusing.

"I mean, have you ever been to an aquarium before?"

"I don't think so," I responded.

Ian looked at me wide eyed for couple seconds, then scoffed. "You'd probably know if you had."

"You're right, I must not have."

"It's like a mini *SeaWorld*, 'cept whales don't splash ya."

"Roger said it was like a zoo for fish."

"More like a prison," said a voice from behind us.

I turned around to see a freckled faced, red headed girl. Her hear was in tight pigtails. She put her hand up for me to shake, but Ian pulled my hand back just as I began to extend it.

"Shouldn't eavesdrop Meg," Ian snorted.

"I wasn't, Kennedy," rebutted Meg. "You just talk too loud."

"Ugh!" was all Ian could muster.

Ian motioned me forward. We both leaned against the seat in front of us. Ian spoke in his quiet voice. "They ain't angel kisses, you know."

"What isn't?"

"The freckles. People with 'em say they've been kissed by angels, but I know better. Especially in her case."

Smiling, I looked back at the freckled faced girl. My eyes looked past them for a moment, and I caught a glimpse of her.

Yes, Amber was on this bus too. Amber was also attending the aquarium today. Amber politely waved at me despite "you know who" sitting beside her.

"You have really unique eyes." Meg moved her nose just a few inches from mine. Caught off guard, I fell back onto my seat.

"Like a liquid blue color," she continued. "I have never seen eyes like that." Now Meg's two friends were examining me as well.

"That's enough. He ain't some attraction at the circus." Ian turned me around, and we leaned forward, as far away from the gawking eyes of Meg as we could.

"She's blunt," Ian whispered. "It can get pretty annoying."

I started to look over my shoulder at Meg who had resumed their normal sitting positions. "No, no!" Ian urged, a little louder. "Don't make eye contact again."

"So now what?" I inquired.

"Avoidance will be our game plan," Ian insisted.

"That doesn't seem very polite."

"Forget manners, Kyle. This is about survival." Ian thought for a moment. "I should know."

"Maybe she'll want to be our friend?"

"Ha!" Ian responded. "With friends like her, you don't need an enemy."

After laughing at his own joke, Ian cleared his throat and looked down at his feet. I watched him, wondering why the sudden pause.

"What?" Ian said.

"Oh, I just..."

"You are nervous. I understand. Probably don't have strange girls like this where you are from."

I just smiled.

"Where are you from?"

"A city. A city far away."

Ian gave me a blank stare. There was a brief awkward moment, and then Ian broke the silence. "Sounds good, one doesn't want to reveal too much about his identity," Ian motioned over his shoulder. "You never know who may be spying."

I nodded in acknowledgement. "Thanks Ian." Ian patted my shoulder.

"That's what pals are for." He waved me closer to him. "Listen, when I get a little, let's say flustered, which isn't often." Ian quickly poked his head up and looked around the bus. I presume to make sure no one was "spying". Then he imparted some words of comfort.

"At these rare times, just take a deep breath and say one word."

I went for my notebook and pen. Ian shook his head. I gave him my undivided attention. "I'm ready."

"All you have to say is," Ian paused to build up the dramatic tension. "Shazam!"

Chapter 29
Fish Whisperer

Ian was truly gifted in the arena of presentation. He even had me keep my eyes closed until we were well inside the building that housed the Aquarium. Other students snickered as Ian led me through the front doors.

"Open!" Ian invited.

"Wow! This is amazing!" I jumped up and down, clapping my hands.

"And this is only the lobby," Ian smirked.

The exhibits in the Aquarium were incredible! The water in the tanks looked so clean, and so fresh. I thought it might be tasty to drink. It was quite a contrast from the murky water that surrounded the light house.

There was so much to see: otters, turtles, penguins and even sharks. I had read about these animals in some of Mary's books. The pictures on the pages did not do justice to seeing them up close and personal. A sort of déjà vu feeling came over me while observing these magnificent creatures. I felt a strange connection to them.

After exploring some of the exhibits, I became increasingly aware of a very peculiar sound, yet somehow a familiar sound. I needed to know what it was.

"Would you happen to know what that sound is?" I inquired of a class mate, standing near me.

All I received from my peer was a blank stare, head shake, and then distance. Literally, the other student took several steps to make sure they were no longer close to me.

I then realized the sound was more of an intense feeling, than an audible noise. So weird. I shook my head, even plugged my ears, but the sound would not subside. I decided to leave my classmates and attempt to discover its origin.

It was like playing the "hot and cold" game Roger teased Mary with, when she was trying to find her car keys. In one direction the sensation would decrease, and when I walked in the opposite direction it would increase.

At one point, the impression became so strong and loud that I thought my head was going to explode. *What is this?*

In front of me, on the cold cement floor, lay a shiny, black stingray. Just a few feet away two boys, hands dripping with water, were laughing and pointing at the sea creature. I gave them a disapproving glare. They gulped and ran away.

Suddenly, the strange sound amplified in my head. My mind attempted to unscramble what seemed to be a message from the stranded stingray. Not waiting for the message to be translated I carefully picked the slippery stingray up and placed it in what was called a "touch pool."

The little ray swam off, out of reach of the anxious children, who were eagerly waiting to pet it.

Pleased with my rescue, effort I gave a sigh of relief and turned around to search for my classmates.

"Next time call one of us for assistance," a lady in an official Aquarium worker uniform instructed. She apparently had been standing right behind me for some time, very stealthy and silent. Maybe she was one of those Urban Ninjas Ian was had told me about.

"Oh, sorry," I replied.

"Please wash your hands and join your class," she said in a matter of fact tone, pointing toward the Boys' Restroom.

I sheepishly nodded and acquiesced to her request.
I washed my hands as instructed, and exited the restroom.

Smiling, I looked around for my class. I widened my eyes, hoping to increase my field of vision. *"Where are they?"* I looked in all directions and didn't see any familiar faces. My smiled fade and my eyes darted back and forth, scanning the crowd again. Still no sign of any class mates. I had lost my group, and I was alone.

Chapter 30
Lost then Found

With no sense of direction I began walking. I came to a hallway lined on both sides with fish tanks. The tanks were full of numberless colorful fish.

While walking down the hallway I had the feeling of being watched, watched by hundreds of tiny eyes. If that wasn't weird enough, I felt I was hearing music, or more like singing.

Pausing at the exit door to the hallway, I closed my eyes to take in the sounds I was feeling. These were pleasant sounds that gave me a sense of peace and contentment; unlike the painful screeching generated from the stingray.

My state of relaxation was abruptly interrupted by a slap on my shoulder. I jumped, and popped open my eyes to find Meg standing in front of me.

"Weird!"

"I'm sorry," I replied.

"Turn around." Meg gently took my waist and spun me around. We both looked at the fish tanks. Every fish was now in the closest corner of their tanks, nearest to me. They were pressed against the glass as if they wanted to reach out and touch us.

"It's like they were following you," Meg said

"Me?"

"Yeah you, I just got here."

"There you are." Ian bounded up to us. "I thought I'd lost you for good."

"Check this out," Meg said pointing at the fish in their tanks.

"Whoa!" Ian surveyed the scene like a seasoned detective. "You didn't tap on the glass, did you? You know you aren't supposed to tap on the glass."

"We didn't, Mr. Goodie-Two-Shoes," Meg said indignantly. "They're following Kyle."

"Really?"

"We don't know that," I said.

Meg stuck her nose into my armpit and sniffed. "Can't be the deodorant."

I gulped with embarrassment.

"You are wearing some right?" Meg continued.

"Do fish even smell?" Ian asked.

"Dead ones." Meg laughed.

Ian and I stood silent, allowing Meg to enjoy her morbid humor.

"Anyways, we best get back. They'll be looking for us." Ian tugged on my arm. "Come on, Kyle. You too, Meg."

We departed, and I gave the fish one last glance. They were all still pressed to the corner, and their music had changed to a melancholy tone. I gave the fish a warm smile and turned the corner.

Chapter 31
Of Fish and Men

Meg, Ian and I finally found our classmates, and our science teacher, Ms. Kate. Everyone was gathered in front of the shark exhibit. One of the Aquarium staff was addressing the group.

"They generally do not live in freshwater," said the Tour Guide, answering a student's inquiry. "Although there are a few known exceptions, such as the bull shark, and the river shark, that can survive in both seawater and freshwater."

"Who cares!" yelled a boy from the back of the group. "Let's see 'em eat something."

The Tour Guide's expression changed from excitement to disappointment.

Our teacher, Ms. Kate's head immediately snapped around.

"Benjamin Jones!" "Front and center."

Students snickered, and a large boy, both vertically and horizontally, came to the front, and stood sheepishly beside Ms. Kate and the Tour Guide.

"He likes to be called D.A.R.," Ian whispered.

"His real name is Ben," Meg interjected.

"Ben sounds nice," I said.

The boy in question had on worn jeans and a shirt, whose sleeves had been recently ripped off.

"Not when the kids call you Big Ben," Ian chuckled silently.

"Why Dar?" I asked

"It's an acronym," Meg stated proudly.

"Like Shazam." "But he ain't no hero," Ian smirked at his own joke.

"Yeah," Meg continued. "D.A.R. stands for Dangerously Armed Rebel."

"He made it up himself," Ian added adjusting his glasses.

"I mean just look at the size of those arms." Meg blushed. "He's got bowling balls for biceps."

Ian and I both looked at Meg who quickly cleared her throat and looked away.

Ben, I mean D.A.R. gave what seemed like a heartfelt apology to the Tour Guide. His face even turned a little red. Perhaps it was because the Tour Guide was a pretty lady, or he was uncomfortable having all his classmates' eyes on him.

Ms. Kate nodded to Ben, and gave him a kind smile. He nodded back, and rejoined the class. All the snickers and chuckles ceased as Ben moved through the crowd of students.

Ian gulped hard. "Someone is in for it."

"In for it?" I asked, puzzled.

"You are so green, Kyle," Meg spouted.

"Easy, Meg. He's new."

"Yeah, that's what green means," Meg rolled her eyes.

"I knew that," Ian stood his ground.

"Oh, here he comes," I cheerfully announced.

Ben looked me dead in the eyes. I assumed the polite response was to smile, so I did.

"Hello."

Ben did not respond.

When Ben passed by, Ian and Meg simultaneously took a step away from me. Ben snarled, and bumped into my shoulder, muttering something into my ear.

Ben went back to his position behind the rest of the class.

Wide eyed, Ian and Meg looked approached me.

"What?" exclaimed Ian. "You didn't just…"

"Why?" asked Meg.

"Never smile at him!" Ian insisted.

"I guess not," I agreed.

"Well?" Meg inquired.

"Well what?" I said.

"What did he say?" Ian asked intently.

"It sounded something like, "Red heat.""

"Don't leave our side," Meg said.

"And we need to stick close to Ms. Kate," Ian added.

"Red heat." Meg shook her head.

I just shrugged. Ian leaned in close. "He said dead meat, not red heat."

"Oh, that doesn't seem very polite."

I abided by my friends wishes, and stayed close to them and Ms. Kate. This made the rest of the morning enjoyable.

We saw some electric eels, river snakes and piranha. Ben was nowhere in sight, or at least I didn't notice his presence.

After filling our bellies with tasty and satisfying bag lunches, the class thanked the aquarium staff and we made our way to the school bus.

"Wait," I exclaimed. "I believe I've left my backpack in the cafeteria."

Overhearing my concern, Ms. Kate stepped in front of me, and put her hands on her hips. "Please be quick about it, Kyle. We're all waiting on you now."

"We'll help too," Meg said.

"I think Kyle is more than capable," Ms. Kate answered.

"Please, Ms. Kate," Ian pleaded.

"Kyle, we'll meet you at the bus."

Ms. Kate escorted Ian and Meg toward the front doors.

I ran back to the spot where I had last seen my backpack, but it was not there. I looked around for a while longer and still my backpack was not in sight. Despondent, I turned to leave and was surprised to find Ben leaning in the doorway. He looked like he was waiting for me.

"Hello, Ben," I said cheerfully.

"DAR, dummy," was his angry reply.

"Sorry," I cleared my throat. "I am new."

"Stupid too," Ben snorted.

Why this young man was so angry, I just didn't know. All I could do was smile at Ben, wondering if someone had recently caused him pain.

"Lost something?" Ben said, holding up my backpack.

I walked toward Ben. "Thank you very much, I can't believe I forgot it."

"You didn't!" Ben shouted. "I stole it!"

"Oh, well thank you for returning it, Ben."

"Quit calling me that!"

"Sorry."

I approached Ben with the hope of retrieving my backpack.

He took a step back, holding one arm behind his back.

"Come and get it, if you can."

Didn't Ben know that was my intention? Why was he backing away while asking me to proceed in acquiring my property?

Chapter 32
Friend or Foe

When I was within a few feet from Ben, he dropped my backpack, and used both his hands to reveal the metal bucket filled with dirty sea water he had been hiding behind his back.

With all his might, Ben hurled the contents of the bucket at me. Something in me clicked. An unseen force or power shot out of my hands toward the oncoming dirty water. The water intended for me splashed back and soaked poor Ben from head to toe.

Ben lost his balance, and his bucket. His feet came out from under him, but before Ben could fall flat on this back, I grabbed him.

It all happened in a split second, but for me it seemed everything had slowed to a turtle's pace. I was able to effortlessly reach Ben, and prevent him from seriously injuring himself. I even caught the falling bucket.

"How?" Ben uttered. He stared up at me, and I simply smiled. "So fast…" Ben mumbled.

We looked at each other for a moment, both trying to make sense of what just took place. I broke the awkward silence. "We better get some paper towels from the restroom."

With wide eyes, and an open mouth, Ben stared at my hands. I held my hand up in front of me. Scales had formed on the outside of my hand, and webbing had grown between my fingers.

"What was in that water?" Ben said dumbfounded.

"Ahh!" I shrieked. "*What is this?*"

Our mutual stupor was abruptly interrupted by the shrill voice of Ms. Kate.

"Kyle Starr and Ben Jones! What on earth are you doing?"

Ben and I walked in front of Ms. Kate, toward the bus. We both kept our heads down. Ben periodically looked over at me. This gave me and an unsettling feeling in my stomach.

Thankfully, my hand had returned to normal. Whatever was on it had dried up and flaked off, and the extra skin between my fingers had retracted. But was my hand really normal now? Or was normal what my hand turned into due to the encounter with Ben? Either way I needed Roger and Mary's help to ascertain what had caused this anomaly.

Something within me was saying that I could trust them; I knew they would still take care of me, even with my malady. I took a breath and continued toward the bus.

Students had their noses pressed against the windows. They watched wide eyed, as Ben and I approached the bus.

When Ben boarded the bus, the other students quickly snickered. My heart became stricken with an uncomfortable pain, a feeling I would later come to identify as "guilt."

Ben sheepishly walked down the aisle, his head hung low. I couldn't tell if it was left over water or tears that ran down his face.

I took a deep breath and put my foot on the first step of the bus. Ms. Kate gently squeezed my arm. "Are you okay?"

Her question caught me off guard.

"What do mean?"

"Bullying will not be tolerated."

"Sorry, Ms. Kate."

"You don't need to apologize, Kyle. I will be talking to Ben and his parents about his behavior."

"It's okay."

"No, it is not."

Ms. Kate smiled and motioned for me to enter the bus. Standing in the aisle, all eyes were now on me.

"Please take your seat, Mr. Starr."

Ian waved for me to join him, but I just smiled at him and nodded toward Ben. Ian dropped his hand and stared at me, with wide eyes

"Can I sit here?" There was no response. I took that as a sign of acquiescence. So I sat.

"I am sorry," I said clearing my throat. Still no response from my seat companion. Speaking in a quiet voice I turned to Ben. "I don't know what happened, but please don't be afraid of me."

"I won't tell," Ben mumbled.

He put his head against the glass and stared out the window. I released a breath of relief and looked forward. Everyone, including Ian and Meg, gawked at me. I did my best to produce a half smile and then closed my eyes.

Once we reached the school, I headed straight for home. I needed to avoid any uncomfortable interrogations from classmates.

I intercepted Mary or Roger on the road, before they could pick me up in front of the school.

"Ya tryin' ta hitch hike today, son?" Roger called from his truck window.

"No, sir."

"Well get on in, unless you plan on walking all the way."

"Thank you, Roger."

Chapter 33
Secret Identity

The ride home was unusually quiet, well at least from my end of things. Normally I would have been asking a lot of questions, and expanding my knowledge base. Today I sat still. Roger sang along to some of his favorite "tunes" on the radio. "Doesn't get much better than this," he kept repeating.

Dinner time wasn't much better for me. My appetite seemed to have fled.

"Okay Kyle, what's wrong?" Mary must have the superpower of intuition.

"Huh?" I shrugged my shoulders and looked at the floor.

"These spuds are amazing!" Roger said, consuming his mashed potatoes.

"Quiet, dear. Kyle is about to tell us something."

"Hmmm," was all Roger could muster with his mouth full of food. Roger placed his fork perpendicular to his food. "Let's have it then, meal's getting' cold."

With her elbow on the table, Mary put her hand under her chin. Her loving eyes looked into my soul. This was it, this was the game changer. "*Courage*", I repeated over and over, in my mind. I closed my eyes, drew in a deep breath, and then stood up from the table.

"I have something to show you."

I walked over to counter and began to fill the sink up with water. Both Mary and Roger looked on with anticipation.

"I hope this doesn't change the way you feel about me. You have been so kind and caring. But if it does, please don't feel bad, I will understand."

I turned off the water and took a nervous gulp. "What you are about to see may shock you. Actually I am pretty sure it will." I stuck my hand into the water filled sink, waited a moment and drew it forth.

"See!"

Roger and Mary looked at each other and then back at me. "Kyle?" Mary was obviously puzzled, but not shocked.

"I don't get it," Roger said shaking his head before he resumed devouring his mashed potatoes.

I looked at my hand...Nothing.

Of course nothing; obviously the water Ben threw at me was dirty. I mean, I had taken baths since the Starrs took me in. Personal Hygiene was an essential part of healthy living, Mary would tell me.

Without thought of the consequence, I grabbed one of Mary's plants off the window sill and dumped it into the sink. Brilliant idea? Mary's face said otherwise, as she gasped.

"Now," I said with a shaky voice.

I quickly stuck my hand back in the water and swished around the plant dirt. I closed my eyes, and removed my hand from the now murky water.

I opened my eyes to meet Roger and Mary's disapproving glares.

"This ain't funny anymore, son," Roger scolded.

Failed again? Too embarrassed and red-faced to be in the presence of the Starrs, I exited the kitchen. Knowing that at least Mary would try to come and comfort me, I decided to flee from the house entirely.

Chapter 34
What Am I?

With a tear stained face, I sat alone on a rock, by the water's edge, and watched a distant ship battle the high waves. What was happening to me? Was I imagining that strange occurrence at the Aquarium? No, I couldn't have, not with the way Ben reacted. I replayed the scene over and over in my mind.

I jolted when I heard Mary and Roger call my name through the fog. I was too despondent to answer their hailing. My only comfort was coming from the sound of the waves crashing against the rocks.

With each droplet of water that pelted me, from the ocean's spray, a strange sensation occurred. I had the feeling that I was closer now to where I was really meant to be. As much as I loved being with Roger and Mary, for some reason the ocean was feeling more and more like home.

I stood up, took a deep breathe, and stepped into the beckoning water.

"No Kyle! Stop!"

Mary ran full tilt toward me; the beam from her flashlight gyrating with each step. Roger was in hot pursuit behind her, with a flashlight of his own; it was moving just as frantically as Mary's.

"Please Kyle, step back," Mary pleaded.

I looked down and realized I was waist deep in the water.

"Get outta there, Kyle!" Roger's request was a little more forceful.

I acquiesced and returned to the shore just in time for Mary and Roger to reach me. Emotionally exhausted, I fell to my knees. Tears streamed down both cheeks. Mary was crying too, and even Roger had moist eyes. In Roger's case, it could have been from running through the wind; he doesn't like to admit he cries.

With arms around both Mary and Roger, I was escorted back to the lighthouse

"Sit Kyle, you are safe now," Mary said as Roger placed me on the sofa. "I will make you some hot cocoa. Roger, please get the boy a blanket."

Roger placed a thick, soft blanket over my back and shoulders. The blanket consisted of a connecting pattern of multicolored squares.

"Mary made this herself for our..." Roger paused and then cleared his throat. "Best get these wet shoes and socks off."

"Thank you," I mumbled. I was feeling awful for causing pain for Mary and Roger.

"Please don't do that again, son. Mary can't take it," Roger said, removing my wet tennis shoes. His gentle reprimand was both loving and stinging.

"I hope you like the large marshmallows, Kyle, we are out of mini." Mary entered the family room with a tray of steaming hot chocolate and cookies.

"Me - oh – my!" Roger held my wet socks in his hands and stared down at my bare feet.

Mary gasped, and the tray of goodies crashed on the floor. I immediately bent forward so I could see past my knees. What about my feet had caused such shock?

Between each of my toes stretched that thin layer of skin, the same skin that had appeared between my fingers with the Ben incident. If that wasn't alarming enough; my webbed toe feet were covered with tiny, soft scales.

Now what? I had read a book about abnormal people sent to perform in carnivals. Was this the fate that would befall me?

Slowly, I looked up from my disfigured feet and studied the expressions of Roger and Mary. I expected to find looks of horror and disgust, but to my surprise Roger was smiling. Mary looked stunned, but not mortified. Roger was the first to break the awkward silence.

"Well, would you look at that?"

Mary put her hand over her mouth.

Roger continued to study my amphibian feet. "Hmmm, let me try something." He disappeared around the corner into the kitchen. I looked away from Mary, and back down at my strange feet. Mary sat down beside me and put one hand on my knee.

With childlike enthusiasm, Roger entered the room carrying a large bowl of water. "Stick them feet in here, Kyle."

"Sir?"

"Do it," Roger nodded. "Trust me."

With trepidation I placed my feet in Roger's bowl of water. Roger then proceeded to wash my feet. In just a few moments the tiny scales, and extra skin between my toes vanished.

"Yes!" Roger clapped his hand with force. "I knew it, it's the salt." Roger grinned at me and Mary. "Don't ya see? This here is fresh water. Sea water is what makes the change."

Mary and I said nothing.

"Say something woman."

Mary choked on her words. "I am not sure what to say."

"Told ya Kyle was special!"

"Of course he is!" snapped Mary. "You are special Kyle. It's just that...well, this is quite unexpected."

"Not for me," Roger proudly said as he rose to his feet.

Having been a seafaring man, Roger said he'd had many encounters with sea folk and sea creatures. Mary, of course, thought her husband was just "spinning yarns."

"I am sorry," I looked Mary straight in her eyes. Mary put her arm around me.

"Oh Kyle, you don't have anything to be sorry about."

"You're darn tootin'!" Roger exclaimed. "Sorry is the last thing you should be. You are a miracle of nature."

"Really?" I sincerely asked.

Mary nodded to the affirmative, and produced a smile that seemed genuine. Suddenly, Roger snapped his fingers at the air. "I'll get my book."

"Dear, let's take it slow," Mary suggested.

Roger was already out of the room when he called back to us. "Let the adventure begin!"

Chapter 35
Myth or Memory

Sitting at the kitchen table, Roger placed a large picture book in front of me. "See!" Roger said, pointing to a picture of a city that seemed to be submerged under water.

I actually couldn't see too well because Roger had turned off the kitchen lights, and we were attempting to read by candle light. Mary said Roger liked to create a certain ambience when he was storytelling.

Roger flipped the page and the next image I saw was a beautiful girl that had a fish tail instead of legs. Her long, flowing red hair covered all of her front. Even so, Mary turned the page abruptly and said, "Next."

Roger rolled his eyes, but acquiesced to Mary's wishes.

"Okay, listen to this." Roger clapped his hands and rubbed them together. "Homo aquatica, also known as Atlanteans, possess many amphibian qualities."

Roger held up his finger. Mary put both hands on my shoulder, and I held my breath.

"The ability to breathe underwater, through the use of twin gills located behind the ear lobes."

I cautiously reached up and touched behind my ears. Feeling nothing out of the ordinary, I shook my head. Roger's sigh seemed to resonate with disappointment. He cleared his throat and continued.

"Ah, ha! Webbed feet and hands provide for superior swimming compared to their surface-dwelling counterparts."

Roger smiled and checked off an imaginary box in the air. I looked back at Mary; she lovingly smiled at me, and then made a funny face in Roger's direction. Mary had a way of making me feel better just by doing the simplest of things.

A few more pages were turned, and Roger exclaimed, "Listen to this! Some sources cite that these humanoid creatures possess the power of telekinesis!"

The room went silent. Roger leaned forward and stared at me, looking deep into my eyes without blinking or speaking. I swallowed to clear my throat.

"Am I not human?"

"Cabbage patch!" Roger playfully slapped the table. "That was not quite what I was thinking."

"But am I?" I insisted.

"Um, I ..." Roger stumbled over his words

"Of course, you are, Kyle, and you are our boy."

Mary softly kissed the top of my head. I almost smiled, but a sudden sharp pain pierced my skull. I fell to the floor, clutching my head as images flashed through my mind.

The first image was of a beautiful woman wearing a crown; she looked like royalty. There was a tiny baby in her arms. She kissed the baby's cheek. When she kissed the baby on the cheek, I felt it on my cheek. It felt so real, I instinctively touched my face.

Next, I saw a young boy swimming fast through turbulent water, with a group of youth swimming closely behind him, smiling and laughing. It seemed as if they were engaged in some sort of game.

Finally, there was a scene that deeply disturbed me. Someone had died. Someone must have been very important, because there was an extremely large group of people gathered in a large, ornate hall. The hall was enclosed by a gigantic bubble. The bubble prevented the surrounding water from coming in. All the attendees were deeply saddened, except for one man.

The unremorseful figure stood in the shadows by a large pillar. He had a sinister grin on his face, and his dark eyes were wide with delight. This man's face haunted me for nights after this episode of delirium, and pain.

Finally, I saw a young boy with his head buried in the shoulder of the beautiful woman with the crown. When the young boy raised his head and revealed his face...it was me!

Was this real? Were these my memories? I didn't recall seeing, or reading anything like this in any of the books I had been consuming. Confusion, and discomfort filled my mind. I gripped my head. *"What does all this mean?!"*

Chapter 36
Sharing My Secret

You don't have to go to school today, Kyle." Mary stood at the foot of my bed.

"But I want to go." I sat up in bed.

"After your, um, vision. You were out like a light."

"Yeah, just take it easy kid." Roger had stuck his head around the corner. "You've had a rough night."

I swung my rocket ship covered pajama legs out of bed. Mary and Roger supported me as I attempted to stand. "I need to go," I insisted. "I need to feel..." We all knew the word I was searching for was "normal."

Roger and Mary drove with me to school. I was a little squished sitting between them in the front seat of Ol'Blue. Their concern for me was palpable.

"I will be okay, I promise." I tried my best to reassure them, but the look on their faces still showed great anxiety.

Mary squeezed my hand and Roger nodded, both attempting to convince me that everything was going to be okay. But I was not convinced.

After the awkwardly quiet ride to school, I was now left to face my peers. Would they sense something different about me? Had Ben kept my secret? Did anyone else know what I was?

What was I? I remained unsure.

I felt both relieved and disappointed, standing in the middle of the hallway, while students passed by me, the occasional smile and hello nods, and a few of the "it's the new guy" stares.

I wanted to feel normal, but I also wanted to feel a bit special too. Perhaps it was my ego or pride, but I wanted desperately to share my uniqueness with someone. Wait! What was I thinking? *Easy Kyle, you are getting ahead of yourself. You don't know what this all means. Just "keep it on the down-low."*

I needed an ally, a confidant, someone I could trust with my secret. Ben inadvertently knew my secret, but could he be trusted to know more?

That's it! I had a "secret identity." Who knew more about such matters than my friend, Ian? Yes Ian, Ian could be trusted, I hoped.

When the final bell rang ending our school day, I quickly searched for Ian. Throughout the day, I had kept mentioning to him we needed to speak after school. I didn't make a big deal about it, and he was as carefree as usual.

Ian was just closing his locker when I came up behind him. "Ahhh!" Ian exclaimed in surprise. "You scared me."

"Sorry, my intention was not to startle you."

"It's cool. My ninja reflexes just kicked in for a minute there."

"May I have a moment of your time?" I inquired.

"Yes professor," Ian replied. "What gives? You're all formal like."

I cleared my throat. "Well, I have something to tell you, or rather show you."

"Cool, what is it?" Ian's eyes lit up. "I like surprises. Will I be surprised?"

"Oh, I think so." I motioned for Ian to follow me. We stepped into an unoccupied science classroom. I put my backpack on the desk and Ian followed suite.

"Is it an experiment?"

"Sort of." I took courage. "Now please keep an open mind." I began to fill an empty beaker with water. "You know how some people have certain abilities, powers?"

"You mean the superheroes?"

"Yes, sort of like superheroes." I handed Ian the water filled beaker. "Well, I think I have some."

"Some what?"

I readied myself and took a deep breath. "Okay, now."

"Dude, I don't get."

"Sorry, I mean now please toss the water at me."

Ian looked at the beaker in his hand. "Are you serious?"

"Very," I assured Ian. "Please proceed."

Ian looked at the beaker of water, then back at me. I nodded my head. Ian shrugged his shoulders. "Okay."

With water dripping down my face, I pondered what went wrong.

"I still don't get it." Ian scratched his head.

"Please fill the beaker again."

Ian turned the tap and proceeded to fill the beaker. "What was supposed to happen?"

"I wasn't concentrating, my mistake. Please count to ten and then toss the water." I wiped the still dripping water from my face. Ian sloshed the water around in the beaker. "Should I count in my head?"

"Yes, thank you. That would be preferable."

Ten seconds later I was wet again. This was beginning to become mildly frustrating, and embarrassing.

"I think I should go now." Ian gently set the empty beaker on the counter. "This is just weird."

"Please, just one more time, I promise."

Ian sighed, and we proceeded with the same routine. This time I stood with my hands stretched toward Ian. I felt ready for the oncoming water.

A smile came over Ian's face. I think he liked my heroic pose. "I believe in you," he whispered. "Whatever it is you are trying to do."

"Thank you, Ian."

I stared as hard as I could at the beaker of water, then I made a humming noise, like Mary does when she is practicing her yoga. I stretched my hands out with even more tension. Ian's eyes lit up. I gave Ian the "go ahead" nod. Ian raised his eyebrows and nodded back at me. I clenched my jaw, gave Ian one more nod of confirmation, and braced myself.

It seemed like everything slowed down; the water coming toward my face, Ian's smile turning into a frown of disappointment as headed toward my face.

"What are you guys do..." Meg burst through the classroom door. She gasped in horror. Ian and I were both startled. We looked at Meg, then at each other, then at something truly remarkable.

The water that had been about to hit my face, was suspended in midair. It wasn't frozen, but it was not moving in any direction. The water was just sort of hanging there, shimmering within its own body.

"How?" Ian's voice cracked. He reached out and touched the suspended water. "It feels alive!"

I took a deep breath and concentrated. With my thoughts only, I willed the water to move toward me. I cupped my hands, and the water gently settled into them.

"Freaky." Ian's voice broke the eerie silence. "Freaky Cool!"

I went to the nearest sink, and let the water escape down the drain. Meg stood at the door speechless. Ian was all smiles. We both looked at Meg, she was about to faint.

"You better come in and sit down, Meg." I gently encouraged.

"Yeah, and shut the door," Ian said firmly.

Chapter 37
Amazing Allies

Meg and Ian sat behind a science desk, and I paced back and forth in front of them. After nervously recounting my Aquarium experience for Meg, and sharing a few new memories with a very enthusiastic Ian, I paused to wipe my forehead with my shirt sleeve.

"Hey!" Ian shouted. "She's writing all this down."

I'd been so wrapped up in trying to express myself properly, I had not noticed Meg taking copious notes in her little, purple diary.

"Meg?" I questioned.

"Stop that!" Ian attempted to snatch her notebook, but it was apparent Meg was used to quickly protecting her precious words from would be thieves. She did have two older brothers.

"This helps me process things, or don't you trust me?"

I didn't know whether Meg's remark was directed toward me or Ian, but Ian answered first.

"You cannot tell anyone, and I mean any one!" Ian was quite adamant. "That is the oath of a sidekick."

Meg stood up, and stared Ian down. "Don't tell me what I can, and can't do Kennedy."

Sensing the tension building, I thought it best that I try a little levity. "Guys, no one is getting kicked in the side, you are both my friends."

Meg and Ian gave me blank stares. I bowed my head in shame and mumbled. "Obviously comedy is not my forte."

After a very brief moment of uncomfortable silence, Meg and Ian resumed arguing. This time they were both standing up, nose to nose.

"Please, listen!" I yelled over the shouts of my feuding friends. "I trust you both. That's why I just shared my story with you."

There was a momentary pause. Ian looked at me and then at Meg. "Yeah, one of us by default."

"That's it, Kennedy, you're dead." Meg pounced on Ian.

Ian and Meg wrestled on the ground. Meg was getting the better of Ian, but I like to think it was because he was being a gentleman, and not really trying to fight back. "Kyle, help me!" Ian screeched.

I surveyed the room for a solution. Mary kept saying, "If you get discouraged, or frustrated, just look up, and the answers will come." She was right.

I closed my eyes, and focused all my concentration on the solution to defuse the rumble. Within moments water burst forth from the all the overhead sprinklers in the classroom.

Meg and Ian's tussle came to an abrupt end. Meg, who had pinned Ian to the cold tile floor, moved off him and stood up.

"What?" Meg stretched out her hands and caught some droplets of falling water.

Ian remained on the floor. He giggled uncontrollably. "Too cool," he said, "too cool." Ian waved his arms and legs across the floor, splashing in the water that surrounded him.

I continued to look up at the sprinklers. Abruptly the classroom door sprung open.

"Whoa!" Mr. Sparks stood in the doorway, his mouth, and eyes wide open.

The instant my concentration was broken the sprinklers ceased. Ian jumped to his feet. Ian, Meg, and I stared at Mr. Sparks. The last few remaining droplets of water fell from the sprinkler heads on to our already soaked bodies.

Moments later, we found ourselves sitting in the principal's office, in front of Principal Stern. Mr. Sparks stood behind us with his arms folded in front of him. Our behavior had not only caused damage to the classroom, but also caused Principal Stern to stay after school, which, as we were told, was not going to bode well with Mrs. Stern, who had dinner waiting.

Principal Stern explained that being tardy for the dinner Mrs. Stern had "slaved over," would make her extremely upset; and when Mrs. Stern was upset "ain't nobody happy."

Ian clenched his teeth, to hold back his laughter. Meg sat in silence, and kept her eyes on the floor.

Even though I had digested many words, sentences, and phrases from all those books I'd read, I couldn't find the right response to the barrage of questions that followed Principal Stern's rant.

Meg seemed so sad, and now Ian didn't look like he wanted to laugh anymore. His nerves had gotten the better of him. How could I let my friends suffer like this? I couldn't. So, I decided to open my mouth, and let whatever would come out come out. I took a deep breath, exhaled and...

Meg jumped to her feet. "I did it." Meg's voice was firm and resolute.

"Excuse me, Ms. McGreggor?"

Meg lifted her chin. "Yes, it was me."

I didn't know Meg that well, but the amount of confidence she was exuding was very convincing and commanding.

"But..." Ian and I were almost simultaneous in our utterance. Meg flashed us a glare. We were rendered speechless with fear, and respect.

"I must say I am surprised with your behavior, Ms. McGreggor." Principal Stern's remark seemed to have a hint of adoration in it.

"As am I," Mr. Sparks added.

Meg looked over her shoulder to address Mr. Sparks. "Well, you know how I like to get those extra credit points."

"Extra credit?" inquired Principle Stern.

"Meg is a straight A student, sir, and the best teacher's aide I ever had," Mr. Sparks said with pride.

"Was there a fire, Meg? I didn't even hear an alarm." Principal Stern's inquiry seemed full of hopefulness.

"No," Meg responded. "Just a failed experiment."

Principal Stern tapped his fingers together and looked past us. "Hmmm, I am leaving this one to you Sparks." We all turned around in unison and gave Mr. Sparks our best looks of remorse and regard.

After a brief reprimand from Mr. Sparks, we took the walk of shame down the hallway. Principal Stern had tasked Mr. Sparks with escorting us out of the building.

"Thank you so much sir for your diplomacy regarding this matter," I said turning to Mr. Sparks, who walked several steps behind us. Mr. Sparks gave me a look of concern, as if I was somehow making a mockery of the situation. He looked to Ian for clarification.

"Oh, he is sincerely serious," Ian clarified. "Kyle talks funny like this all the time."

"Oh?" said Mr. Sparks.

"Well, I mean funny different, not joking funny," Ian added.

"I understand," Mr. Sparks nodded.

Ian wiped his brow, and gave a smile as a sign of relief. Meg shuffled along, keeping her eyes on the ground; not quite the courageous young lady we witnessed just moments ago.

"My mom doesn't need to know, right?" Ian pleaded.

Mr. Sparks smiled. "No really damage done," he said, "Nothing our trusty custodian can't handle."

Ian elbowed me in the ribs and whispered, "The janitor is crazy."

Mr. Sparks cleared his throat. "Ian."

Ian blushed. "Sorry."

We exited the school, and Mr. Sparks stood in front of the double doors with his hands on his hips. "Everyone better head straight home now. And I hope you all dry off before you get there."

Chapter 38
Bonds of Friendship

Meg definitely deserved praise for protecting my secret. I gently touched Meg on the shoulder.

"Thank you, Meg, that was very brave of..."

Meg spun around abruptly and watched Mr. Sparks enter the school. As soon as the doors closed behind him, Meg collapsed to her knees and began to sob.

"Meg, I am so sorry. I did not mean to scare you with the display of my ability to manipulate the properties of water."

Ian snickered. "Wow, what a mouthful."

Meg to broke into a bit of laughter. "It isn't you," she insisted. "I hate having to lie, especially to people I respect."

This gave me pause. I had no idea the "art of equivocation" could cause the propagator so much pain. Mary was always saying honesty was the best policy. I thought her philosophy was for the victim's protection. Now I knew that our actions and words affected all parties involved, even the source.

Was I then to tell the world the truth about myself? I didn't even know what all of this meant, or even what I really was.

I sat down on the sidewalk beside Meg, and cautiously touched her shoulder. "You are a trusted friend, and confidant Meg; I don't want to hide anything from you."

"What?" Ian blurted out.

Meg raised her head, and wiped her tears with her shirt sleeve. "There's more?" Meg sniffed.

I nodded. Ian shrugged his shoulders, and sat down on the sidewalk with us. After taking some effort to cross his legs, he unexpectedly and unreservedly put his arm around Meg's shoulder. In the adolescent world we refer to this gesture as a "half hug," a step used in the initial stages of courtship.

Surprisingly, Ian's action didn't frazzle Meg. "Here," Ian said handing Meg her journal. "You left this on the floor." Meg managed to produce a sincere smile as she took her book from Ian.

"The cover is a little wet, but I think the inside is still good." Realizing what he just said, Ian had a moment of panic. "I mean, I guess it's good inside, I didn't look or nothin'!"

Meg held her journal tight and quietly whispered, "I know."

Ian's eyes widened. "You do?"

I stood up, and resolutely said, "Well, do you two want the privilege of seeing what else I am capable of, or not?"

Ian and Meg both looked at me with concern. I think I had just come off as arrogant, which was really masking my nervousness.

"Pardon me," I said, as I rubbed the back of my neck. "I mean, it would be my privilege to share more about myself, with the two of you, my dear friends."

Even though Ian and Meg simultaneously smirked, I felt better about my revised invitation. Meg hopped to her feet first and extended her hand to Ian who was struggling to get up. Once Ian had his footing, Meg quickly released his hand. I looked at the pair with inquiring eyes. Meg glared back. "What?"

"Umm..." was all I could say. I wanted to inquire about the true nature of their relationship, but I wasn't sure who to ask.

"So, where we goin'?" Ian stammered before I could formulate an innocent inquiry.

"Do you have a bathtub?" I asked.

"Duh, who doesn't?" Ian responded.

"Wonderful, then it's off to your residence Ian."

Meg, Ian and I began walking in the direction of Ian's home.

"Oh, and salt," I said emphatically. "We'll need lots of salt."

Chapter 39
Bath Time

Ian's mom was waiting in the open door way. "Ian Frances Kennedy! Where have you been?"

Meg and I looked at each other, then at Ian.

He frowned at both of us.

"Mom is a big musical fan, okay!"

Meg chuckled, but I didn't understand the reference. I had familiarized myself with the DC and Marvel Universes, and even Image, Dark Horse, and IDW, but Frances from a musical wasn't registering. My blank expression prompted Meg to nudge me, and whisper in my ear, "Seven Brides for Seven Brothers."

Still nothing, but I was intrigued. Not only was I intrigued about this multi matrimonial song and dance themed entertainment piece, but I was also intrigued regarding the way I felt when Meg's lips had softly touched my ear. I felt a twinge of jealousy; Ian had something very special, and he didn't even know it.

"Hey!"

Ian's shout snapped me out of my pontificating, inner monologue. "You guys comin'?" Ian was already inside the house, standing beside his mom, and waving us in.

"Be polite, son."

Meg and I entered the Kennedy's lovely home. Mrs. Kennedy squeezed Meg's arm. "Nice to see you again Meg."

"You too, Mrs. Kennedy."

"Hello, Mrs. Kennedy," I said, extending my hand. "It is a pleasure to meet you."

Mrs. Kennedy gave me a firm, but kind hand shake and looked deep into my eyes. "Genuine, I like that," she said. "I can always tell if someone is being honest with me. Can't I Ian?"

"Yes, Mom." Ian walked down the hallway, and into the kitchen.

"Thanks, Mrs. Kennedy. My name is Kyle Roger Starr."

"Oh," her voice rang with delight. "So, you're the famous Kyle."

My face flushed.

Mrs. Kennedy squeezed my arm. "Thank you. Ian is actually starting to read Shakespeare now."

"Mom!" Ian's shout of embarrassment echoed through the house. "Please stop."

Mrs. Kennedy smiled, and waved Ian's pleas away. "Really Kyle, you have been a good influence on my son. Thank you."

Humility felt good. Mrs. Kennedy's words left a lump in my throat; all I could do was smile at her. Meg was Mrs. Kennedy's next target. "And you Miss. Megan."

Meg's eyes widened, and she took a step back. "You have taught Ian love..."

"Mom!" This was Ian's most adamant yell so far.

With full composure Mrs. Kennedy concluded her remark. "...the love of science."

"Oh," Meg said, with a growing pinkish hue on her face.

Mrs. Kennedy took mine and Meg's hands in hers. She gave them a gentle squeeze. "I am just grateful Ian has such good friends." She paused and turned to Ian, waiting for him to respond.

"What?"

"Well?" Mrs. Kennedy was waiting.

Ian paused for a moment, and then looked at the kitchen floor. "Yeah, yeah good friends."

His mom sighed, and Ian walked briskly out of the kitchen carrying a large, clear canister. It was full of small, white granules. "You guys comin'?"

Mrs. Kennedy turned to Meg for clarity. "Science experiment," Meg clarified.

As we all made our way upstairs Mrs. Kennedy called after us. "Just be careful."

We filled the bathtub with warmish water, and then dumped the entire contents of the jar into it. I was ready for my big reveal.

"Okay, now what you are about to witness may shock you so be pre..."

"Get on with it already!" Ian's impatience could not suffer any of my preambles.

I blew out several breaths of air, and began to put my foot in the water.

"Whoa!" Ian interjected, "Are you keeping your socks on."

"Oops!" I was a little embarrassed, and perhaps more nervous than I realized. My pant legs were already rolled up, but I had neglected to remove my socks. Sitting on the edge of the tub, I began to remove my socks when I felt a hand placed on my shoulder. I looked up at Meg.

Her smile helped calmed my nerves. "It's okay. We're your friends."

Ian peeked over Meg's shoulder, and gave an approving nod.

With socks now off, I was ready to take the plunge, per se. I looked at Meg and Ian one more time, for comfort. They both smiled and nodded enthusiastically.

With that I stepped into the tub. I closed my eyes for a moment, and then looked at my feet. Nothing felt really different, so I raised one foot out of the water. It had not changed.

"I don't understand?"

"More salt?" Ian asked.

"I don't believe so."

"What then? Water too warm?"

"Ian stop," Meg cut him off from further questioning.

"What? I am just trying to ascertain which variable might be off." Ian smiled at me with glee. I think he was hoping I would be impressed with his articulate response. I was.

However, the perplexing nature of my current predicament mitigated the enthusiastic response Ian seemed to be hoping for.

Meg scraped her finger on the bottom of the empty canister. She was able to get a few white granules to stick on the end of her finger. After a close examination, she licked the end of her finger. "Cook much?" Meg said to Ian.

"Huh?"

"Taste this."

Ian scrunched up his face. "Eww."

"Not my finger dork. Get your own sample."

Ian tentatively scrapped some of the white substance out of the canister. With a shaking finger he administered his own taste test. Immediately his grimace turned to a smile. "Whoops," Ian gave me a cheesy grin. "At least you're a little sweeter now."

Meg simply groaned.

Chapter 40
Transformation

Attempt number two.

We drained and refilled the bath tub. Ian suggested we dump salt in the water from every possible container in the house, just to narrow any margin for error.

"It looks like the Dead Sea," Meg remarked.

"Like you've been there," Ian quipped.

Before Meg could banter back, I cleared my throat.

"Uh hum, I am ready, again."

Meg and Ian instantly became silent. Both gazed at me with great anticipation. Courageously, I stepped into the water; instantly I felt a change taking place.

I took a deep breathe, to steady my nerves. It was time to test the bonds of friendship.

"Ready?" I inquired.

"Of course," said Ian. "Let's see this already."

Working to keep my balance, I lifted my right foot out of the water.

"Whoa! I mean super whoa!" Ian was ecstatic.

I saw the reflection of my scaled, webbed, shiny foot in Ian's extremely wide eyes, and breathed a sigh of relief. Then I looked at Meg; she was paler than usual.

"Meg?" Ian and I said in unison.

She wobbled a little before plopping down on the toilet. Thankfully the lid was closed. I got out of the tub, and kneeled in front of her. She put her hands on my shoulders. Her gesture was encouraging.

"I'm good," she insisted. "I just didn't expect... well..." Meg nodded toward my feet.

"Sorry," I stood up, and submerged my foot back into the bath tub water.

"Don't be. You are who you are, Kyle," Meg said in her most sincere tone.

"Thanks, Meg."

"This is awesome!" Ian was giddy with excitement. "What else?"

Wanting to be sure it was okay to continue, looked at Meg, she nodded.

"Well, if it doesn't offend anyone. May I remove my shirt?"

"Just leave the pants on, okay?" Meg was doing her best to keep a sense of humor.

I handed Ian my shirt. "Here goes."

I sat down in the tub. *I hope salt comes out of denim. I don't want to upset Mary.*

Holding my breath, I submersed myself in the salty water. I was not sure how long I was under. It seemed effortless to deprive myself of breathing in air from the atmosphere. I must have been under for a while because both Meg and Ian had open mouths, and shocked expressions on their faces when I emerged.

The water trickled off me as I slowly rose to my feet. Meg and Ian seemed to be frozen in speechless awe. I swallowed hard.

"Please, someone say something."

"May I touch it?"

The first words out of Meg's mouth caught me off guard, to say the least.

"So beautiful," she said, reaching her hand toward me.

Gently, Meg ran her fingers through my hair.

I shivered unexpectedly.

"Like silk," Meg turned to Ian. "Come on, Ian, touch it."

"I'm good," Ian replied.

Meg's hand stopped behind my ear, and she gasped. "What is this?" Meg turned my head. "Ian, look at this!"

Now Ian was all in. Literally, he joined me in the tub.

"Oh man! This is incredible."

"What? What is it?" I had no idea what was causing Meg and Ian to examine me this way.

Meg looked me in the eyes. "You don't know?"

I shook my head.

Meg looked at Ian, and the two of them drug me out of the tub and placed me in front of the bathroom mirror.

Now I was seeing what they had been so enamored with.

SILVER, my once black hair was now silver. Not blonde, not even white, but silver.

"Look behind your ears," Ian suggested.

Meg held my hair back. I tried to turn my head to see, but my peripheral vision wasn't quite that good.

"Here, just feel this," Meg guided my hand, and I touched, what felt like slits behind my ear.

"What is it?" My voice trembled.

"I am pretty sure they're gills," Meg said.

Ian put his arm around my shoulders. "You …are the man!"

"To be honest, I am feeling like a freak."

"No!" exclaimed Meg, "Different can be beautiful."

"Different? He is more than just different. He is a freakin' Super Hero!"

Coming from Ian that was probably the highest compliment a friend could ask for.

So there I stood, silver hair (silky and beautiful according to Meg), webbed toes and fingers, gills behind my ears, and oh yeah, thousands of tiny scales covering my body.

What was I? This was a real conundrum. My next thought was, "*I hope when I dry off, I resume my former appearance, or I will definitely have a lot of explaining to do when I get home.*"

Chapter 41
Minor Meltdown

Yes! It worked. I was now dry, and the effects of the salt water had worn off. I borrowed a pair of Ian's sweats, since my jeans had been tossed into Mrs. Kennedy's dryer by Meg. Ian had distracted his mom, so Meg could complete this stealth operation.

Thankfully Mrs. Kennedy didn't notice that I was departing her house in different pants from those that I arrived in, or at least she didn't say anything about it.

We decided to reconvene later at the lighthouse, because Ian's mom insisted he eat some dinner, and Meg needed to check in with her parents.

It seemed like no time at all before Meg was at my kitchen table enjoying a homemade cup of cocoa and good "chinwag" with Mary. Ian was in the TV room with Roger. They were engaged in an intense conversation about my origin. Roger had several thick historical, mythology, and encyclopedia books spread out on the table.

Of course, Ian had several comic books lying on the table adjacent to Roger's books. Ian was attempting to help Roger understand the difference between two underwater characters; Aquaman and the Submariner.

Mary and Roger were very accepting of the fact I had entrusted Ian and Meg with our secret. Mary and Roger said they trusted me, therefore, if I trusted my friends, they would trust them too.

While the gentlemen were trying to determine my possible next of kin, Meg and Mary were discussing legends of mermaids. Meg asked Mary if she ever thought I'd grow a fish tail. I sensed the question bothered Mary, as it did me. Mary, in polite manner, replied, "I really don't think so dear."

Actually, the whole situation was bothering me. A strange feeling began to churn in my stomach. It was an emotion that I knew I had experience before, but I just could not remember.

Everyone in the lighthouse seemed to be talking about me as if I wasn't even present. My head began to ache. The voices of Roger, Ian, Mary and Meg grew louder and louder, each overlapping one another, especially Ian's voice. The cacophony became too much for me to bear.

"Enough!" I shouted. "I am right here!"

The room went silent. What was I doing? Had I lost my mind? Part of me wanted to just be quiet and let the moment pass, but there was another part of me that had to be heard.

"No Meg, I am not growing a tail anytime soon!" My voice was still loud, but now shaky. Everyone just stared at me. Funny, no one told me to calm down or lower my voice. At least I didn't hear anyone attempt to.

"As for you, Ian, I am not some fictional character in your colorful little books."

As I surveyed the room I was met with a disappointed gaze from Roger. Meg and Ian had deep looks of sadness in their tear-filled eyes.

I couldn't even look at Mary, I knew that I had crossed the line. A look of disapproval from her would have crushed me.

"I am just a boy, a normal boy, and I wish all of you would stop treating me like a freak." With that I made an exit to my bedroom and slammed the door.

I pulled the covers up, rolled over in my bed, and stared at the wall. In the darkness, I could hear sounds of shuffling in the next room, and then soft exchanges of good-byes before a door closed.

I'd read about children receiving spankings for such unruly behavior, or even having their mouth washed out with soap. Was this my impending fate? Soon the door to my room opened, and Mary's silhouette appeared on my bedroom wall.

"Here it comes." Tears rolled down my face and I listened to the soft footsteps of Mary approaching. She sat on the side of my bed and gently put a hand on my back.

"You don't have to talk if you don't want too. Roger has taken your friends home." Mary's voice was calm. "All of this must be very frustrating for you." How could Mary remain so sweet and calm?

Mary softly patted my back. "The thing is, Kyle, you are not just a normal boy. You are an incredibly special boy, our special boy."

Now I was crying even more.

Mary stood up. "Try to get some rest. We love you Kyle. Good night." Mary softly closed the door.

This was the worst sleepless night I had since coming to live with Roger and Mary. I was racked with grief and remorse for the terse words I had spoken to Ian and Meg. Lying in my bed, staring up at the dark ceiling, my mind raced. Would Ian and Meg ever forgive me? Had my rude deportment cost me the friendship of two wonderful peers?

The morning sun broke through my window and bounced across my face. I scrunched up my eyes in reaction to the bright light. I knew I had drifted in and out of slumber, because now I was recalling my nightmares of Ian and Meg ridiculing me in front of the whole school. They threw salt water filled balloons at me and screamed, "Kyle is a freak!"

As I became more cognizant, I realized that I wasn't worried about my secret being kept; I was concerned about losing the bonds of friendship that had been forged.

Rubbing my eyes I stumbled into the kitchen still in my train PJs. "Mornin', Kyle," Roger cheerfully greeted me. "Mary's got another amazing hot breakfast ready for ya."

Stunned, I sat down at the kitchen table. "Here we go," said Mary, placing a steaming plate of pancakes, dripping in golden syrup, before me.

Where was my reprimand, my scolding? Had Alzheimer's set in? Were they just choosing not to remember the events of last night?

"Eat up now, Kyle," Mary encouraged. "You want to make it to school on time."

I couldn't help smiling. Roger and Mary knew I felt sufficient guilt, and they didn't see any need to add to it. I was so lucky to have them in my life.

Chapter 42
Custodian Confidant

Apprehensive to ride the bus, Roger generously offered to take me to school in Ol' Blue.

At one point, he dangled the keys in front of me, and asked if I'd like to "take 'er for a spin." He thought his joke would calm my nerves, but Mary wasn't amused. Needless to say, Roger drove.

The ride was over before it even began. I sat in the idling truck, staring at the school. "Let me give you a hand son," Roger said. He leaned passed me, and opened my door. I looked at him, then back at the school. Roger gave me a loving pound on the shoulder, followed by an encouraging wink and a half smile. I knew his subtext meant, "Take courage, you can get through this."

"You can do this, Kyle!" I encouraged myself, ready to approach the front doors of the school. By now most of the students had filed in. When the double doors closed behind me; I paused before looking down the long hallway.

My first class was the infamous Mr. Mon's class, with Ian. I gulped and proceeded down the hall. "Time to face the music," I whispered to myself. Wait. There really was music. More like whistling, but very pleasant, and calming. I stopped by a set of lockers to listen.

"Nice, isn't it?" I said to a couple students getting books out of their lockers. They gave me a strange glance. A young girl walked in my direction. She was bopping her head and doing a sort of dance/walk. "What song is this?" I inquired of her. The girl stopped and pulled two stringed plugs out of her ears. "Hi?" she said.

"Oh, hi," I said. "I was wondering what song they are playing for us?"

She scrunched up her face. "Song?"

I blinked nervously and pointed up. "Yes, over the um, speakers, or I guess the proper term is intercom?"

She stared at me for a moment. "Dude, there's nothing playing." She put her plugs back in and skipped away.

I was perplexed. What was I hearing? The whistling music seemed to grow louder. I did an about face and began to follow the music to its source. The whistling sounded like hypnotic waves on the sea.

In a trance like state, I followed the sound through several hallways and down a flight of stairs. I stopped in front of a door at the far end of an empty hallway. The door was labeled "Janitor." Under the Janitor label was white piece of paper with the words, "Old Man of the Sea," written on it in colorful crayon.

I don't know how long I had been standing outside the door, but the whistling music had stopped. Without thinking of the consequences, I reached for the doorknob. Before I could touch it, the door slowly opened with a sustained squeak.

When the door finally came to rest, I was greeted by The Janitor. The same Janitor Ian mentioned was "crazy;" however, I felt comfortable in his presence. I didn't sense that he was insane, or that I had anything to be afraid of.

"I was wondering when you'd stop by, Kyle."

My mouth dropped open, the Janitor just winked and smiled. He nonchalantly offered me a seat. I closed the door to the closet sized room and sat down on an overturned bucket. Looking across the room at this intriguing, elderly man, I wondered why I wasn't afraid.

"You know me?" I inquired of my host.

"I know of you," he said pointing to an air vent in the ceiling. "It's amazing how sound and voices travel."

"Excuse my bluntness, sir, but who are you?"

The elderly gentleman chuckled. "You may call me Jonah. Most folks call me Mr. Salt, or the crazy one."

"Oh," I said, not sure how to respond.

"Water," Jonah said, pointing to an unopened plastic bottle, on a shelf beside me.

I turned and reached for the bottle.

"No, no," Jonah said softly. "Just watch."

I sat back and Jonah closed his eyes. He stretched his hand toward the bottle. After a few moments, the water inside began to slowly stir. Jonah clenched his jaw and closed his eyes even tighter. The water in the bottle spun around at a furious rate, and then suddenly the bottle tipped over. Jonah let out a deep sigh, and his whole body seemed to relax.

"How?' I exclaimed.

Jonah removed his cap and wiped his brow. "Phew," he puffed. "Like riding a bike, kinda."

I looked at Jonah dumbfounded. "Now, Kyle," he said, "I think you know how."

I felt warmth in my chest and my heart pounded. "You are like me!" I shouted. Before I knew it, I was giving this stranger a hug.

"Easy now," Jonah cautioned. "These bones are very, very old."

"How old?" I spoke without thinking. "Sorry, that was rude of me."

Jonah leaned back in his chair. "Ha, the Starr family have taught you well."

"Does this man know everything about me?"

"Yes," Jonah said. "And I don't know why you confided in those two school mates of yours."

"Wow!" I sat on the edge of my chair. "Did you just read my mind?"

Jonah grinned and a sharp pain shot across my forehead. I doubled over in agony. The pain was so intense, I fell to my knees. Just as I was about to lose consciousness, Jonah put his hand on my shoulder.

"You will be all right," he said. A wave of calmness passed over me. My violent headache instantly ceased.

"You've let your abilities lie dormant for too long now."

I heard his words, but his mouth wasn't moving.

"Whoa," I blinked my eyes. "This is strange."

I slumped over and shook my head.

Jonah stood up straight. "Let me show ya something."

Jonah walked over to a shelf, stepped on a little stool and took a worn, dark blue book off the top level.

I watched with anticipation. Jonah shuffled back to me, and plopped the book on my lap. I wiped some thick dust off the cover, hoping to see some words or at least a picture but nothing

"Go ahead, open 'er up."

Chapter 43
Life of Jonah

Jonah pulled his stool over next to me and nodded to the book. When I flipped open the cover, I saw a picture of Jonah standing beside an elderly woman. The caption under the picture read: "10 Years of Heaven."

"Is this your wife?" I blurted out.

Jonah cleared his throat and pointed to a date written on the corner of the picture, 1967. Jonah looked exactly the same age now as he did then. Jonah turned the page for me.

"That was the Widow Wilson, before we got hitched of course." Jonah's eyes glistened. "These are my children, grandchildren, and even got me some greats."

We continued turning the pages which were full of pictures of Jonah with different families. There was even a picture of Jonah at some sort of ceremony, he was wearing a dark robe, and had on a funny hat.

I ran my fingers over the words "Papa is a Doctor." under the picture.

Jonah stood up and looked out the tiny window in his small room. The sun was shining through and bouncing off the dust particles in the air.

"Are you okay, sir?" I inquired.

"So much livin'," Jonah smiled. "Life has been wonderful."

I closed the book, stood up and joined Jonah. "I have lived a long time away from our home under the ocean. Most of my powers have left me over time, but bein' by the sea kept a few active."

"So, we are both from…"

"Atlantis." Jonah's eyes glistened, as if remembering a pleasant memory for his past lives. "Yes Kyle, yes we are."

Jonah and I sat in his little office for what seemed like hours. He gave me a brief history of Atlantis, and how it didn't really fall into the sea, but the sea swallowed it. Over time its forbearers evolved, and adapted to their new environment.

He said Atlantis was always a place of wonder, power, and what we now call, magic. That is why the inhabitants were able to survive when their great city was covered in water. Not only survive, but flourish and live on from generation to generation.

When I asked Jonah the obvious question of why he left, his reply was simple, love. Love drew him away from Atlantis, and love kept him here.

Jonah politely told me he must get on with his work, but that I was welcome to visit him again. I still had so many unanswered questions. Jonah didn't want to talk anymore. He either didn't know the answers I was looking for or didn't want to reveal them to me.

Upon parting, I asked one last question. "Do you know who I am, or rather who I was in Atlantis, and why I am here?"

"That's a pretty long question, Kyle." Jonah scratched the side if his face. "This I can tell you. We learn from our past, but we don't have to live in it. The reason you are here is up to you."

I did not find solace in his answer, but I left graciously. What an amazing experience! It was like a beautiful, lucid dream.

Chapter 44
A Clean Slate

After blinking my eyes several times, to clear my foggy mind, I realized I was standing in the same hallway where I first heard the music. The scene seemed identical to the one I was in before the whistling led me away. The girl with the plugs in her ears was just skipping away from me. How could this be? Hours had past. Hadn't they?

Surveying the hall, I listened carefully for the clarion call of Jonah. All I heard was the slamming of lockers, and the squeaking of shoes.

Disappointed, I made my way to my first class. To my surprise, Ian's seat was empty. I looked around the room, and he was nowhere to be found.

I had really blown it; one friend down, and one to go. I hung my head in shame, and sat down in my desk.

With a sigh, I began to remove items from my backpack. The others students were engaged in idle chatter. There was no teacher present in the room.

"What an obnoxious jerk I was," I mumbled to myself. Obviously, my rude behavior had caused Ian to either change classes, or even worse, forgo the precious opportunity to attend this institute of higher education, and no longer drink from the fountain of knowledge.

Even the initial excitement from my conversation with Jonah was now fading. I felt sick to my stomach, not the type of "junk food' consumption sickness, but a deep emotional pain. Just then, there was a slap of papers on my desk. Comics! I had never been so happy to see a stack of comics.

"This is the New 52." Ian slid into the desk adjacent to mine. "Here, you'll probably dig this one."

Ian held up a Superman comic. "He's like you, arriving alone in a new land, and adopted by some pretty awesome folks," Ian whispered.

I graciously accepted the comic, and looked into Ian's eyes, attempting to gage his demeanor. Ian just smiled, and began to explain the difference between the former DC Heroes and the Revamped Heroes.

"At first, I was bugged, but it's cool now that Sup keeps his undies on the inside. Mom is happy too. She says Halloween will be less embarrassing for her now."

Ian was going on as if yesterday's tirade had never taken place.

I could understand the Starrs being able to forgive me, but my peer? Ian was mature beyond his years.

Soon, Ms. Nash, a substitute teacher for Mr. Mon, entered the room. She was a pleasant looking, middle aged lady, with a delicate laugh. Ian said she was "all ite," but of course "not the Master we were looking for."

Ian, and I had a delightful time in class; he even walked me to my next period, and enthusiastically said he'd see me at lunch. Lunch, this would be my test of friendship with Meg.

Since the Aquarium trip, she had taken occasion to join Ian and I for lunch at our designated table.

The cafeteria was buzzing with the usual prattle, gossip, and bantering. Sometimes, I find eavesdropping on the various conversations fascinating. Mary was not particularly supportive of my aloof, elusive observation practice, but she said if it was for educational purposes, she would not show too much disapproval. She did however give one caveat; no repeating what I had heard, not even to her.

Ian took a break from his eloquent speech about "The Hero's Journey" to consume his sandwich. I laid my lunch in front of me on the table, but I didn't have much of an appetite. While Ian chewed, I listened to the students around me. I was hoping I would be able to pick out Meg's voice in all the chatter.

"Trade you a piece of my dad's chocolate cake for some of those homemade cookies." Meg's voice was loud and clear.

"Well?" she said just as loud. Then I realized her voice was coming from directly behind me.

"Huh?" I spun around. Meg had caught me totally off guard. Not that we hadn't made trades before, but I thought Meg was going to give me an intellectual thrashing.

"You know you love this cake," Meg said as she sat down. "And don't worry..." Meg spoke in an imitation whisper. "I won't tell Mary."

"Sure thing!" I exclaimed. After all, her dad was a baker.

Meg and I participated in our traditional lunch time bartering ritual as we proceeded to eat. Watching Ian and Meg act with no guile toward me caused a lump to grow in my throat, and the absence of animosity toward me created tear-filled eyes. Meg noticed before Ian did. She gave me a nudge and a subtle nod, and then mouthed the words, "clean slate."

I knew then, that all was forgiven.

"So, what are we going to do after school today?" Ian inquired, with a mouthful of sandwich

"Swimming," I confidently announced. Ian and Meg just stared at me. "Well, aren't you as curious as I am?"

Meg cautiously nodded, but Ian exploded with enthusiasm and threw his hands in the air. Ham flew out of his sandwich and landed on an adjacent table. Ian turned to see where his missing lunch meat had gone.

"You can go ahead and keep that, it's on me." Ian addressed the girls at the table that had received his flying ham.

The girls weren't amused, but we laughed hysterically, probably more than we should have. It felt good to laugh, really laugh. I think it released any last bit of tension all of us were trying to keep hidden.

Phew! A potential disastrous reunion turned out to be a confirmation of true friendship.

Chapter 45
The Kiss of Life

Ian and Meg stood at the edge of the pool. They watched with bated breath as I approached the end of the diving board. I was about to embark on my next great adventure.

"Should we be doing this here?" Ian whispered to Meg. Meg surveyed the surroundings of the indoor public pool. "He won't transform. This is fresh water, remember? We just wanna see how fast he can swim."

"I know, I know, but I'm still nervous." Ian bit his fingernails intensely. He chewed faster and faster with each step I took toward the end of the diving board

Ten feet seems a lot higher when you were above the water looking down. Perhaps I should have just hopped in from the edge of the pool, but I wanted to make a dramatic splash for Ian and Meg. I owed them that.

"You can do this Kyle," I said under my breath.

Looking over at Ian, who was now clutching Meg's arm, didn't boost my confidence level. What did I have to be afraid of? Apparently, I was indigenous to water. Shouldn't the clear blue H2O below be beckoning me to plunge in? But all I was feeling was trepidation. Perhaps it was the fear of the unknown.

"Hey kid, are you ever gonna jump or what?" came an impatient voice from behind me.

When I turned around, I saw "Big Ben," I mean D.A.R., I mean Benjamin Jones. He recognized me and froze. I could tell he was as equally surprised to see me as I was him. Ben's mouth gaped open for about half a second, and then he screamed.

I took a step backward and fell off the diving board.

"Whoa!" My limbs flailed in the air.

Wide eyed, Ben looked down at me.

SLAP! My body hit the water with such force, I was rendered unconscious. During this I had another vision, slash dream, of a magnificent underwater city.

The city was surrounded by some sort of protective bubble. The people on the outside of the bubble were swimming in the water, and those on the inside of the bubble were walking like normal land folk. A strange feeling of home sickness overcame me, but it was for a home I was struggling to remember.

This feeling was soon replaced with an overwhelming sense of joy. Something soft, and wet pressed against my lips.

My eyes slowly opened to a blurred field of vision. I could make out an image of a female leaning over me.

Meg? She had come to my rescue, and given me the "kiss of life," and I had loved it.

"Wait." I couldn't do this to my best friend, Ian. He cared deeply for her, and I was sure she would reciprocate the feeling, if only Ian was to proclaim his affection for her.

In shame, I turned my head to the side. I rubbed my eyes and blinked. There was Ian and Meg side by side staring at me in amazement.

"Are you okay, Kyle?" an angelic voice said. I looked up and I saw her. Yes, Amber, the Beauty. Even the light behind her cast a heavenly glow on her wet, but still silky hair.

"Amber," I couldn't help but produce a goofy smile. "Thank you."

Amber, Ian, and Meg helped me to me feet. My eyes were locked on Amber. My knees were weak, and I had rumblings in my belly. Later, Roger told me it was called being, "smitten," like he was, the first time he laid eyes on Mary.

"We can take him from here, Amber," Meg insisted.

"Are you sure?" Amber said.

"Yeah, we'll get him home."

"Okay. Well, let me know if I can bring him something."

"Will do!" Ian affirmed.

I watched Amber as long as possible, until Ian and Meg dragged me out the pool facility doors. She gave me the most warm, tender smile I had ever received. Now I knew everything was going to be all right.

"Why?" I asked Meg.

"Quit pouting, it's for your own good."

"She's right, man," Ian added. "Take a look."

We all looked back to see Amber's beefy boyfriend, Brad interrogating her.

"What do you think you're doin'?" Brad snapped.

"My job!" Amber retorted, before she stormed off.

Brad flashed us a quick glare, and then proceeded to follow Amber. Ian and Meg recoiled, but I was still in a daze of happiness. I let out a sigh and put my hand over my heart. Ian snickered. Meg made a vomiting sound and stuck her finger in her mouth.

"Sick!"

Ian looked at Meg. "Someone's got it bad."

Meg turned a little flushed, and quickly avoided eye contact with Ian. Ian snickered again. "Yeah," Ian raised his eyebrows. "Real bad."

Chapter 46
Young Love

Who's aching for some bacon?" I gleefully proclaimed, opening the door to Roger and Mary's bedroom.

"What the Sam Hill!" Roger shouted.

Mary slowly rolled over. "Kyle? Are you okay?"

"I'm fantastic!" I held my tray out toward Roger and Mary. Roger sniffed the air. "Is that...?"

"Yep! Bed and breakfast, just for you."

I was so excited to present the ones I loved with this magnificent feast. Mary sat up, and picked up her alarm clock. "Kyle! It's 5 a.m.!"

"Early bird gets the ..."

"Where's my orange juice?" Roger interjected examining my tray of scrambled eggs, bacon, and toast.

The Starrs graciously declined eating breakfast in their room. Perhaps I should have included fresh squeezed orange juice. Once seated around the kitchen table, Mary and Roger stared at me with a curious fascination. I happily kept consuming my portion of the delicious meal I had prepared.

"Are you sure you are okay, Kyle?" Mary asked.

"Glorious," I replied with a mouth full of egg and toast.

"He's got it."

"It?" Mary asked Roger.

"The bug," Roger replied.

Mary quickly leaned forward and felt my forehead. I gave her a huge smile. Roger chuckled. "No darling, the other bug," Mary glanced at Roger, then back at me. I was still grinning.

"Kyle?"

"Yes Mary?"

"Are you... I mean, do you like someone?"

I nodded my head vigorously and took another bit of breakfast. Roger cleared his throat. "Wait for it."

I swallowed. "I'm in love!"

Roger pointed his fork at me. "Bingo."

Mary sat back in her chair. "Wow, I had no idea."

Gaining her composure, Mary sat up straight, then reached over and gave my hand a squeeze. "So, who is the lucky girl?"

Roger interjected, "My money's on Beauty."

I looked heavenward and sighed. "Amber the Beautiful."

Roger clanked his knife and fork together. "Bingo again!"

Mary playfully slapped his hands. "Stop that."

I abruptly stood up from the table and stretched my arms out. "Well, this has been wonderful. I better get off to school now. Punctuality is a quality desired in a suitor."

Mary and Roger looked at each other dumbfounded. I gave them both another cheesy grin, and proceeded to my room.

"How did you know?" Mary whispered to Roger.

Roger stood up and kissed Mary on the cheek, and whispered in her ear, "Because that's how I looked when I fell for you." Mary blushed as Roger put their dishes in the sink.

I returned to the kitchen with my hair combed back, teeth brushed, and backpack over my shoulder. "Shall I drive today, Roger?"

"Ha!" was Roger's reply.

Roger and I bounced up and down on the truck's seats, as Ol' Blue sputtered down the road toward school. I periodically checked my hair in the mirror. "Can she go any faster Roger?"

"She can go plenty fast Kyle, but a speedin' ticket would only make you late for school? Did you wanna be late?"

"Hmmm." I muttered.

The closer we got to school, the more my knees knocked together.

"Nervous?"

"No sir, just excited to start another day of learning."

"Hog wash! I know nervous when I see it."

I gulped hard, not knowing what to say. Roger parked Ol' Blue in front of the school. He turned off the engine and gave me a stern, but loving look.

"I've been where you are Kyle. My Mary is the love of my life." For some reason my eyes became wet. Roger continued. "I ain't saying Miss. Amber is the one. I mean you guys are still kids, but you'll never know if you don't give it a shot."

I scratched my head.

Roger chuckled. "I am saying don't let your nerves get the best of you. Take courage, and follow your heart."

Roger patted me on the back. I exited Ol'Blue, and watched Roger drive away. Something in me changed. I felt deep concern for Amber and her happiness. Was this more than mere adolescent infatuation?

With this thought running through my mind, I made my way through the labyrinth of students, crowding the hallways. Standing by my locker were my two trusted companions.

"Hi guys," I pleasantly said.

"Don't do anything crazy today," Ian warned. "Brad holds grudges. I speak from experience."

"I'm fine Ian. How are you?"

"No time for small talk Kyle," Ian insisted. "Once these meat heads choose their target," Ian quickly surveyed the hall, before finishing the statement. "It's say goodbye to your mommy time."

"I'll be okay. I still have the memory of our osculation to give me courage."

"Your what?" Ian said.

"He means her life saving kiss," Meg said sarcastically.

"Oh," Ian said with a snicker.

"Correct you are, my astute friend," I said to Meg, giving her a pat on the back.

Meg grabbed my arm, rather forcefully. "Seriously Kyle, she isn't worth the beat down."

Just then Amber came around the corner. We all watched as she went to her locker. She was a good twenty feet away, but I felt like she was right beside me. I smiled at Meg. "Yes she is."

Confidently, I walked toward Amber. *"Courage Kyle, courage,"* I said in my head as loud as I could.

Ian bit his nails and Meg shook her head in despair.

"Hi, Amber." My voice cracked, just a little.

Amber was genuinely surprised to see me. "Kyle! Hi." She ran her finger through her hair, which caused one knee to go weak. "How are you doing?"

"Are you happy, Amber?"

"What?"

"Sorry, I mean I hope you saving my life hasn't put a burden on your relationship with Beefy, I mean Brad."

Amber giggled. What was I saying? And why was I saying it? I guess it was because I cared about her, not just liked her.

She blushed a little.

"You're sweet." I guess I blushed too. "Brad can be intense sometimes, but..."

"Why then?" I interjected. Ooops. It was too late to retract my question.

"Why do I go out with him?"

I just smiled. We looked at each for a moment in silence. "Hmmm," she said. "I am beginning to wonder."

I was enjoying the beginnings of a smile when the still forming grin was wiped off my face by a violent slam against the lockers. I crumbled to the floor.

Everything around me was fuzzy. I blinked until my vision restored. I saw Meg marching toward Brad with Ian in tow. Meg yelled something, but the ringing in my ears prevented me from clearly hearing her. It must have been pretty bad by the look on Ian's face.

And I am guessing from the way Brad stepped back in shock, Meg's screaming was what Roger would say were, "fightin' words."

Chapter 47
When Push Comes to Shove

Stop it, Brad!" I could hear Meg loud and clear now. "You need to grow up!" Meg reached down and touched my forehead. I thought it a strange gesture, until I saw Meg's hands.

She looked at her blood tipped finger. Her entire body shook, and her red face turned a shade redder. "Jerk!"

I covered my ears. Ian must have sensed what was going to happen next, because he ran toward Meg, but it was too late; Meg did the unthinkable. SLAM!

Meg shoved Brad into the locker.

"Whoa!" Ian was as stunned as I was.

Through tears, Amber tried to intervene. "Brad, please don't!"

Even Amber's heartfelt plea wasn't enough to restrain this bully. Brad pushed Meg back. From all the books I had read, this was considered cowardly behavior.

Brad was the size of a tree and Meg petite, like a flower. So, it didn't take much effort for Brad to knock Meg off balance. Unfortunately Meg tripped over me, and landed with a thud on her backside. She immediately looked up at Brad, indignant.

Amber couldn't take anymore. "Meg's right, Brad. You're a jerk!" Amber ran down the hallway crying. Brad waved her off, and turned his attention back to Meg. He pointed at Meg and laughed.

"No!" came a primal scream from Ian.

Brad turned to face Ian, who was now running full speed toward him. Brad straightened up, and cocked his fist, like a cobra ready to strike. Ian kept charging toward Brad with his fists flailing in front of him.

One of Roger's favorite saying popped into my mind. "The manure is about to hit the fan."

My two best friends were putting their health, and well-being at risk by defending me. I had to do something. *"Quick Kyle, think."* Time seemed to slow down, and the idea hit me like a bolt.

I focused all my mental power on Brad

Mid swing, Brad found he couldn't move. He was frozen like a statue. Ian took advantage of Brad's momentary pause and pounced on him. Ian's fist found Brad's right ear. The punch, which was more like a slap, probably hurt Ian more than it did Brad.

Regardless, Brad flew back into the locker. Wide eyed, Brad was pinned against the locker.

A crowd of had gathered around, blocking off the hallway. The students had formed a square around Ian and Brad, like a boxing ring.

Ian stood in front of Brad, his fists, and voice shaking. "You...you want some more of this?"

Brad didn't move. He uttered a quiet, "No."

"What?" Ian shouted at him.

The crowd of students gasped at Ian's taunt. "I said... no." Brad's voice was quivering. Ian relaxed his fists for a moment, then abruptly raised them again. "You got something you wanna say to my friends?"

"S... s... sorry guys." Brad coughed out.

"Now, get outta here!" Ian shouted, puffing out his chest.

Brad cautiously slid down the row of locker, moving away from Ian. Students cheered and jeered, watching Brad briskly make his exit from the hallway. Applause echoed in appreciation for Ian's heroics.

Meg and I helped each other to our feet. Meg stared deep into my eyes.

"What did you just do?"

I stepped back and shook my head, looking anywhere but into Meg's eyes.

"Me?"

"Spill it. I know you did something."

I leaned close to Meg and whispered in her ear. "The human body is made up of 70% ..."

"Water," Meg finished my sentence.

We looked at each other and smiled.

"Please don't tell Ian," I said.

"No, I think we should let him have his moment."

Meg gave me a wink, and I sighed with relief. She joined the throng of newly formed Ian fans. I stood back and watched. I was happy for Ian, yet worried about Amber.

"What's going on out here?" A mature voice boomed over the cacophony of the crowd.

It was Principal Stern. He marched down the hallway toward us. The students parted. It reminded me of Moses parting the Red Sea. Yes, I read that one too.

"Back to class!" Principal Stern bellowed.

Ian and Meg got swept away in the dispersing sea of students. I turned and tried to make my escape too but was halted by a hand on my shoulder.

"Let's see it," demanded Principal Stern. I reluctantly took my hand off my forehead, and exposed my injury.

"Who?" he insisted.

"I fell against a locker."

Principal Stern stepped back and put his hands on his hips. "I know a fight crowd when I see one Mr. Starr. Now who were you brawling with?"

"Sir, I didn't hit anyone. My head hit a locker." I was becoming quite skilled in the art of equivocation.

Principal Stern wasn't buying it. "I will ask one more ..."

"It was Brad, sir." a forlorn, but still angelic voice spoke up from behind me. I turned, and my heart skipped a beat. "Amber?"

"Brad started it. Kyle was just talking to me and..."

"Thank you for your honesty, Miss. Dawson," Principal Stern turned to me. "See the school nurse, Kyle."

"May I walk him there?"

Principal Stern looked us both over. Amber had a soft innocent smile on her face, and of course I had an over enthusiastic grin.

"Will that help, Kyle?"

"Oh yes, sir!" I replied. "That will help very much."

"All right then," Principal Stern acquiesced. "You may walk together."

"Thank you, sir," we both said in unison.

"Now, I have the pleasure of tracking down Mr. Barker." Principal Stern left, mumbling under his breath.

Walking beside Amber felt like I was walking on clouds.

"I am sorry I left," she said.

"It's okay Amber." How could I possibly be upset with her?

"I guess I just got scared. I'm not good at confrontations. My parents..." Sadness filled Amber's voice.

"The important thing is that you came back." I gave Amber a sincere smile. "Thanks."

Amber shook her head and frowned.

"Brad had no right to do that. He's always so jealous, and possessive."

"That must be hard for you, Amber." Now I was applying a technique Mary taught me called "validation."

Amber giggled. "You know you say my name a lot."

"Do I, Amber?"

We both stopped walking. Amber ran her fingers through her hair. "Yes Kyle, yes you do."

"I guess it's because I really like the way your name sounds."

Amber's eyes twinkled. "Thanks, I like hearing you say it."

My sincere smile now was a cheesy grin. Amber brushed my hair aside and gently touched the laceration on my forehead. I hoped my sigh of pure bliss wasn't audible because inside the butterflies were in complete chaos.

"We're here," Amber said, motioning to the nurse's office door.

"Already?" My disappointment was palatable.

"I'll see you tomorrow Kyle."

"Please," was all that came out of my mouth.

Watching Amber walk away left me with a lonely feeling. We had made a real connection, and I didn't want it to end.

Chapter 48
Healing Balm

I'm calling his mother, right now!" I'd never heard Mary so upset. "He is a brute!"

"Please Mary, I really am okay. In fact, I feel wonderful." Mary removed the cold cloth from my wound. "You need stitches."

"Really, I'm fine."

I really didn't feel any physical pain though. However, my heart did ache a little. I knew it was from, what the books call, "separation anxiety."

Mary threw the cloth on the kitchen table. "No, Kyle! You are not fine." She marched back and forth across the kitchen at a feverish pace.

"Sweet heart..." Roger put his arm around Mary's waist. "Please sit." Roger pulled a chair out for her. "I'll make cocoa, everyone loves my cocoa."

Mary put her head in her hands and wept. My eyes blinked uncontrollably, and I too began to cry. I reached out and touched Mary's hands. "Please Mama, don't cry."

Mary looked up and embraced me with a hug I'll never forget. "I just love you so much, I don't want to see you hurt." This moment will last with me forever. Without pretense, Mary and I expressed our genuine affection for each other.

"Wow! That is a deep cut!" Roger exclaimed, breaking up our tender embrace. "What did that school nurse of yours have to say about it?"

"Uhhh," I responded sheepishly.

"Kyle? You went, didn't you?" Mary's inquiry was more of a rhetorical question.

"Well, not exactly." I knew manipulating the truth wouldn't work with Mary.

"Why?"

I gulped, fearing I might be in trouble. "After Amber touched my head the pain went away."

"The power of love." Roger smiled and continued with his cocoa preparations. Mary sat back in her chair.

"Indeed," Mary agreed.

I just sighed in contentment.

Roger placed his famous marshmallow, and whip cream cocoa in front of Mary and me. "This is perfect honey," Mary's anger was dissipating. My enjoyment of the beverage was stifled a bit, due to Roger examining my laceration.

"I wonder?" said Roger.

He kept muttering something on his way to the sink. Mary and I turned to see what he was up to. We watched Roger pour an entire salt shaker into a glass of water; he turned around and grinned at us.

"May I?" Roger asked, holding up his glass of salt water, and a wash cloth. I nodded with approval, and anticipation.

"Dear, do you really think..."

Roger plunged the entire wash cloth in the salt water solution.

"It's worth a shot ain't it?"

Roger applied the soaked wash cloth to my head. It only took a moment before Roger stepped back, and in his booming voice announced, "It's bubbling like hydrogen peroxide!"

I was impressed with Roger's knowledge of the healing arts. Mary stood up and joined Roger. They both examined my head. "Honey, please fetch me a clean cloth," Mary instructed Roger. "Please dampen it just a little."

Mary leaned over my shoulder. "I am going to clean the wound now, Kyle. Let me know if it hurts."

Roger handed Mary the fresh, wet towel. She began to tenderly wipe away the congealed blood from my cut.

"Ouch!" I exclaimed.

Mary gasped and jumped back. "Are you okay?"

I giggled. Roger immediately burst out laughing. "Good one kid."

Mary shot us both a disapproving glare. But I knew she was trying to keep her composure, and not laugh too.

"Sorry," I said bowing my head, hoping my attempt at humor hadn't caused offense.

"Will you look at that!" Roger yelled.

Mary gasped and put her hand over her mouth. She took a step back. Her eyes were wide, full of surprise and disbelief.

"Did it work?" I timidly asked.

"Feel for yourself," Roger said. He put my hand where the cut was supposed to be. I felt some tiny, oval shaped ridges where my laceration had been.

"No way!" I exclaimed.

"It's a miracle Kyle," Mary said clasping her hands together. Mary kissed me on the forehead. "I always said you were special."

Falling asleep that night was easy. Mary and Roger loved me for who I really was. Could nothing surprise them? However, in the all the excitement of the day I forgot, or maybe subconsciously, neglected to tell Mary and Roger about my encounter with the Janitor.

One thing at a time, I justified.

After closing my eyes, I dreamt how my life was all fitting together. I had loyal best friends, loving guardians and even the most beautiful girl in the world had given me a kiss. Yes, I was counting the resuscitation as a kiss.

Chapter 49
Something in the Air

There was an atmosphere of exuberance at school this morning. Making my way to my locker, I saw pockets of giggling girls pointing at various boys who walked passed them. It seemed they were all involved in some sort of covert planning sessions. I retrieved my books for the day and turned. I came face to face with Meg. Literally, our noses touched. We both laughed nervously.

"Oh, hi Meg. Uh, sorry about that."

Meg brushed her hair to the side of her face and looked down at the ground. "No apology necessary." Meg slid her foot in front of her in a sort of semi-circle motion. I was sensing something. How could I say this politely? There was something, well, odd about Meg this morning. She seemed a little tense and apprehensive. I thought I better defuse the awkwardness with a question.

"Our fellow students seem to be to exhibiting unusual behavior this morning." I paused for Meg's response but she said nothing. "I mean, there seems to be a heightened level of joviality, especially amongst the female population."

Meg took a deep breath. "Kyle, I was wondering ..."

"Guys, you'll never guess what!" Ian blurted out; interrupting what I felt was going to be some tender words from Meg. Meg sighed and leaned against the lockers. Ian paused, looked at both of us with curiosity, shook his head and continued. "Anyway, I've been targeted!"

"Targeted?" I asked.

"He means asked," Meg clarified.

"Oh," I said, still unsure of the context of the conversation.

"To that!" Ian announced, taking my shoulders and spinning me around. I still didn't see. Ian saw my puzzled face. He pointed to a large, hand-painted, paper sign hanging above our heads.

"MORP?" My mind scanned the catalogue of information I had accumulated from various resource materials such as, the Merriam-Webster Dictionary, eight of the 32 books in the set of Encyclopedia Britannica, and a wonderful website called Dictionary.com. There was no reference for this MOPR.

"I don't ..."

"It's when the ladies ask the dudes to the dance," Ian quickly interjected, saving me from my ignorance.

"Oh," I said. "That is an interesting alteration from custom."

Ian and Meg both stared at me. After a brief pause, Ian snickered and slapped me on the back. "You crack me up man."

"I apologize. My observation was not intended to cause you discomfort."

"Ha!" Ian chortled. "There you go again."

Meg sighed with a roll of her eyes. Not in a condescending way, which I had been the recipient of before, this time there was something almost pleasant in her reaction.

A group of young men, with matching t-shirts with the words, "Math Rules" on them, walked by us. One of the gentlemen called out, "Hey Lego, how you doin'?"

Since he was looking in my general direction, I responded. "It's Kyle, actually. Nice to…" The gentleman scoffed and shook his head, continuing his stride. Ian was shaking his head too.

"They were charmin' on Meg." Ian informed me.

Meg's face turned a slight shade of red.

I must have looked pretty perplexed, because Ian continued to explain.

"They call her Lego my Mego." I was still puzzled.

"You know," Ian insisted. "Like the waffle commercial."

I just smiled, feigning understanding. I had, on occasion enjoyed consuming Mary's homemade waffles, but I was unfamiliar with the advertisement Ian was referencing.

To cover up my ignorance, I said something that I thought was clever. "Perhaps they would be worthy of your affection, Meg."

"What?" Ian's words reverberated down the hallway.

"For the MORP ceremony," I continued.

Meg's shade of red turned a chalky white. Her eyes even began to water.

"Are you alright?" I inquired.

"I need to leave." Meg turned abruptly.

She rounded the corner before I could even say, "See you at lunch".

I turned to Ian who was shaking his head. "For a smart dude, you're kinda clueless when it comes to the ladies."

"What do you mean?"

Ian shifted his posture before going into his teaching me lessons of life stance. "Well, for one..."

The school bell rang, cutting Ian short.

"Whoa, gotta bail on ya, Kyle." Ian cocked his head to one side and shook his finger in the air. "Ms. Murphy doesn't take kindly to tardies." Ian grinned, pleased with his impersonation. "See ya at lunch." Ian flung his backpack over one shoulder and sprinted down the hallway, weaving in and out of passing students.

I closed my locker and proceeded to my first class. Today I wouldn't reunite with Ian and Meg until the trading of our edibles at the cafeteria. I was having a difficult time concentrating during the three classes that preceded our lunch break. I really wanted to know what Ian meant by "clueless when it comes to the ladies."

Chapter 50
The Invitation

L unch could not have come any sooner. Even though I loved Biology, Geography and Ceramics, those classes could not reveal to me the secrets and rules of being a teenager.

My knees bobbed up and down while I sat in anticipation at our designated lunch table. When were my two friends going to arrive? I kept looking at the cafeteria clock, and back at the door to the cafeteria. "What is taking them so long?"

I set my lunch items out in front of me in my usual orderly fashion. Finally! Meg came through the door. Strangely, she hesitated when we made eye contact.

Usually she smiled and enthusiastically bounded over to our table. Why was she looking around the room? Surely she saw me. Wait, she is turning to leave. I stood up ready to shout across the room, but just then Ian saddled up beside her. Taking her by the arm, he escorted Meg toward our table. Meg's frown turned to a look of anger. There was no getting away from Ian though, and a moment later Meg stood in front of our table.

I gave Meg a genuine smile, but she did not respond in kind.

"We must be in a multiverse," Ian said pulling Meg down to sit beside him. "I was just hit again!"

I became concerned. "Brad?"

"What? No. The ladies love the Ianmister."

"Who?" I said directing my question toward silent Meg. She just looked down at the table.

"Maybe it's the shirt." Ian tore open his shirt and buttons flew everywhere.

"Hey," Meg finally spoke. "Knock it off."

Students around us pointed and laughed. Ian just nodded his head and grinned. "You see," he said, puffing out his chest and rubbing the shiny, metallic textured Big Red "S", centered on his equally shiny blue t-shirt.

"Wow! That looks authentic," I said with enthusiasm.

"Of course, it is," Ian replied.

"No one can resist the Man of Steel, right Meg?" I joked.

Before Meg could respond to me, if she was even going to, Ian leapt to his feet and put his hand in the air, with his palm facing me. "My man!"

I knew exactly what to do. I had witnessed this ritual many times during the sporting events Roger relished watching. "You da man!" I shouted back at Ian.

A teacher politely asked Ian to clean up his buttons, and for me to eat my lunch without any more outbursts. I guess with Ian's flying buttons, and hand slapping we were pushing the limits of acceptable lunch time behavior.

"What did I get myself into?" Meg mumbled as she spread out her lunch.

"Are you okay, Meg?" I asked in all sincerity. She just pointed to her mouth, which was suddenly full of food, indicating that she wasn't going to respond.

Ian snickered and unpacked his lunch.

"Ian."

"Yes, Kyle."

"Your earlier unfinished comment has left me in a bit of a quandary."

"What comment?" Ian said.

"You said, I quote, clueless when it comes to the ladies."

Ian stared straight at me in fear. Meg was glaring at him. "Well, I, um…" Ian looked down at his green Jell-O and began poking it with his fork. "You know, I don't really…"

From seemingly out of nowhere, four Red Rock Rooster cheerleaders jumped up beside our table. One of the girls said, "Hit it!" and music began to play.

All the cheerleaders pointed to me in unison and sang, "Two, four, six, eight, Amber wants to take you on a date! Go, Kyle!"

At the conclusion of their rousing performance, which Ian was still bobbing his head to, the girls handed him an oversized card. The card was a magnificent sparkly home crafted masterpiece; the brilliance even rivaled Ian's t-shirt symbol.

"Lucky," Ian said, opening my card from Amber.

"To say the least," I said. "This is amazing. Does this mean she wants me to escort her to the dance?" I was asking the cheerleaders, perhaps to spread further joy to my fellow students.

"Of course, she does, dummy," Meg's statement was sharp, not in her usually playful way.

"Meg?" I was searching for the subtext behind her words.

"Congratulations," Meg said. I don't think she meant it though, because she stormed off, neglecting to collect her partially eaten lunch. I looked over at Ian for answers. He was grinning even more than usual.

"Awesome!" Ian was jubilant for me. "See Kyle, dreams do come true. It's like Mom says, you just gotta believe."

Chapter 51
Paging Doctor Starr

What an amazing feeling. I was exuberant. The most beautiful girl in the school wanted me to take her the girl's choice dance.

"This is incredible!" I said, skipping down the hallway.

Yes, I received some sneers and eye rolls from my fellow student, but I just did not care.

As I skipped merrily along, I caught a glimpse of a picture, out of the corner of my eye. I recognized a face in the picture, so I stopped. In a cabinet, behind glass was a picture of Meg and her math team. The picture was in front of a trophy that read "Regional Champions."

My exuberance dimmed a little as I thought of how odd Meg acted at lunch. *"She's fine."* But was she? Was I the cause of her discontent? I needed answers, I needed sage advice. It was time to visit my mentor. It was time to converse with Jonah the Janitor. I can't let this feeling of joy be extinguished by something that could be nothing.

After knocking vigorously on Jonah's door for several seconds, I was greeted by an unfamiliar face. "May I help you?" a middle-aged woman said.

I took a step back. "Oh," I paused and looked at the sign on the door, just to make sure I was inquiring at the correct place. The label Janitor was there, but no sign with the words, "Old Man of the Sea."

"You okay pet?" the lady said. She spoke like one of the women from Mary's Jane Austin movies. I looked at the name patched on her gray shirt.

"Yes Maggie, I was just wondering if..."

"If Mr. Jonah was here?" Maggie jumped right in.

Phew, I thought for a moment that my encounter with Jonah was going to turn out to be just a lucid dream. I smiled big. "Yes. Is he in the vicinity?"

Maggie cocked her head to one side. "He said you were very proper."

"He told you about me?" I was getting a little nervous.

"Mr. Jonah informed me that if his young friend came inquiring, I was to tell you not to worry. Mr. Jonah is visiting a granddaughter up north." Maggie thought for a moment. "Or was it a great granddaughter. Ha, I can never keep it straight with him."

"Thank you, Miss. Maggie." I bowed graciously.

"Hold on a titch." Maggie disappeared around the door. I stretched my neck, attempting to see what she was doing. She returned with a small conch shell in her hand. "He left this for you."

"Thank you," I said, examining my gift.

"Mr. Jonah will return in a week. You can thank him in person." Maggie gave me a pat on the shoulder. We said farewell to each other and I tried my best to exit eloquently. I think she appreciated my attempt at sophistication, until I stumbled backward on the stairs. She just shook her head and smiled.

"Where does he get 'em," she mumbled.

Alone and slightly embarrassed, I walked into the cafeteria just as lunch was ending. I was not a thief, so I am not sure why I did it, but before I knew it I was walking back to my locker with one of the lunch room salt shakers in my pocket. I was breathing heavily, and needed to calm down. I took the little shell out of my pocket and put it to my ear.

It's true what they say; it really does seem to produce ocean sounds. Hearing familiar sounds released the tension I was feeling, and to my surprise and delight, the shell did even more. Listening to the shell caused my senses to heighten.

An unexpected sound was being produced via the conch. I could hear moaning; someone was in pain. The shell was acting like an amplifier. I followed the sound until I came to the Men's Locker Room, and cautiously entered.

Now the moaning sounded like it was being produced from a bull horn. I removed the shell from my ear, and could still hear the moaning, although now it was more of a faint murmur. I turned the corner and discovered Big Mike. He was sitting slumped over on a bench, wearing his football outfit. I gulped hard and turned to leave.

"Cool shell," he said, looking at my hand. "Me and my kid sis used to collect them along the beach in front of your lighthouse."

"Thanks," I timidly replied. "It was a gift."

Big Mike gripped his knee with both hands, and leaned his head back, wincing in pain. "Nice," he said through his gritted teeth.

It was obvious he was in tremendous agony. Mary had taught me the art of validating the feelings of others, so I thought I would put her lessons into practice.

"You seem in a tremendous amount of pain," *Good start* "I am surprised you are not more upset."

"Say what?" was Big Mike's bewildered reply. Ooops, Mary made conversing with others seem so easy.

"Do you have a game today?"

Mike looked at his clothing, and then up at me. "Practice, this is just my practice gear."

"Oh, I better depart then. Good talking to ..."

"No worries, little man," Big Mike broke in. "It ain't for an hour."

I cautiously sat down at the end of Big Mike's bench. He gave me a nod of approval. My nerves calmed down and I gave him a half smile in return.

"I applaud you for you desire to be so punctual."

"Ha," Big Mike laughed. "You are one funny lil' dude Kyle."

"Thank you, Mr. Mike, or should I call you Mr. Big?"

"Mike is just fine," Big Mike said, producing a big teeth filled smile.

Even though my comment was sincere regarding his punctuality, I liked that Big Mike thought I had some sense of comedic timing.

That was one of the many skills I admired in Roger. He always kept Mary smiling and laughing. In fact, Mary said that was one of the many qualities about Roger that made her to fall in love with him. Perhaps I too could use this skill to woo Amber.

"Ahhhh," Big Mike's outburst interrupted my drifting thoughts.

I looked at Big Mike in alarm.

"I am so sorry, Mike. What happened?"

It took a moment for Mike to compose himself. I sat awkwardly, awaiting his response.

"The usual," he groaned. "Had my legs taken out from under me during last week's game."

I instinctively looked at Big Mike's legs. I knew they had not literally been "taken out," but as I said, I was looking out of impulse. I had come to realize that the use of metaphors can give one pause.

"Ahhh," Big Mike groaned again.

"Mike, you are in a lot of pain. Let me get the school nurse. Perhaps she can give you some of her ointment?"

Big Mike gritted his teeth. "I'm not gonna use her's you sicko."

Big Mike smiled at me through his pain.

"I'm sorry," I muttered.

Big Mike gave a pain-laced laugh. "It's from a movie."

"Oh," I said. "Sounds intriguing."

"It's a riot." Big Mike closed his eyes and scrunched up his face.

"Laughter is a wonder medicine," I stated. "I wish we had that film now."

"Ha!" Big Mike bellowed as he gripped my shoulder tight. Now I was beginning to feel some pain myself.

"Little K, you crack me up."

"You too, Mike." I rubbed my shoulder and winked.

"Ha!" Mike slapped me on the back. "There you go again, funny guy."

Chapter 52
Salty Solution

Big Mike released my shoulder and slumped forward putting his hands on each of his knees. He let out a large, sustained exhale. "Phew," Big Mike's eyes were wet. "I hope I can do this."

I put my hands in my coat pockets and shivered. Big Mike's distress gave me the chills. I wanted so badly to alleviate his ailment. Wait, in my pocket, the salt shaker. Did I really foresee I would need this precious mineral? Who cared; I thought I could heal Big Mike, so I was going to go for it.

I produced a nervous laugh and shifted on the bench. After all, I was taking a calculated risk talking to a prominent member of the school society. "Of course I'm not a licensed doctor, but I do know some homeopathic remedies."

Big Mike just stared at me.

I cleared my throat. "Homeopathic means..."

"I know what it means Kyle. I'd even accept a placebo, if that'd work."

"Okay then," I said. "I just need to get my hands wet."

Big Mike looked straight in my eyes and nodded. "I trust you, Kyle. There is just something about you."

I found a foam cup by the sink and proceeded to fill it with cool water. "This better work," I thought to myself. I took the pilfered salt shaker and shell out of my pocket and gave a sigh of gratitude.

"Did you tell me to take the salt?" I said to the shell.

"Say what Kyle," Big Mike called out.

"Coming." I said over my shoulder.

I approached Mike with my saltwater filled cup; I had dumped the entire contents of the shaker in, just to be thorough.

"Okay, you ready, Big Mike?"

"Did you use soap?"

I gave Big Mike an awkward grin. He smiled back, probably sensing that I was nervous.

"This is going to seem a bit strange."

"Well, let's get strange then."

"It's probably best that you keep your eyes closed."

Mike gave me an "are you kidding" look.

"Please," I pleaded.

"Whatever, you're the doc," Mike let out a calming breath and acquiesced to my request.

With Big Mike's eyes closed, I took a deep breath and poured the water out of the foam cup onto my hands. The change was instantaneous. I clamped my transformed hands on Big Mike's injured knee. Mike twitched.

"I shall now proceed," I announced in my most doctor like voice. Mike, with eyes still closed, grinned and nodded.

I closed my eyes and began to concentrate on alleviating his pain. I wasn't feeling anything but awkward. I opened one eye to peek at Big Mike, he was keeping his eyes closed, but had a concerned look on his face. My mind began to race.

"Come on, Kyle, you can't let Mike down."

Anxiety overcame me and I began to shake. Big Mike put his beefy hand on my shoulder.

"Relax, kid, you got this."

He let go of my shoulder and leaned back against the locker.

A soft, pleasant, woman's voice echoed through my head like a distant memory.

"The power is within you. Now let it out."

I repeated her words over and over. "The power is within you. Now let it out."

"Ahhh." Big Mike broke my focus with a painful groan. I immediately lifted my hands off his knee. "No, no keep goin', Kyle. It's a good pain."

With Big Mike's approval I resumed his treatment. I felt a force like water, rushing through my body. I sensed Big Mike's injured knee healing.

An hour later; I sat on the bleachers, and watched Big Mike sprint down the football fielded, he periodically gave me a thumbs up.

There was power within me, power to help others, but why? I still didn't know the whole truth about my origin. It was time to go deeper, deeper into the sea.

Chapter 53
Aquatic Alliance

The salty spray from the crashing waves caused each of us to blink. Standing beside me at the water's edge were my faithful friends, Ian and Meg. They were the first I told about the healing of Big Mike's knee.

Actually, they were the only people I had told. Mary and Roger would have definitely forbidden me to do what I was about to do next.

"Are you sure about this, Kyle?" Meg's voice was full of genuine concern.

"Should have brought my Super 8," Ian mused.

"Are you crazy?" Meg snapped. "We can't film this. That's incriminating evidence."

"I wouldn't let it fall into the wrong hands, Meg. I'm not an amateur." Ian gave me a nod of assurance. "Kyle knows I've got his back."

I nodded. "Like any dynamic duo would."

Ian's eyes widened, and he smiled with delight.

Meg rolled her eyes at my use of Ian's vernacular.

Their concern for my welfare was touching and tender, as always. But this time I was confident, there was no need for alarm. I knew what I was doing. Again, Mary and Roger just would not approve.

The sun had set. We had found the most secluded area of the beach, for the next step in my evolution. I took a deep cleansing breath and put one foot into the water. "Thank you both for being here," I said looking over my shoulder.

"Are you sure we shouldn't have told the Starrs?" Meg asked.

"We will, Meg, just not now." I hoped Meg would relax and enjoy this moment. She kept looking up and down the beach while shuffling her feet nervously in the sand.

"Shhh Meg, let Kyle do his thing. We can't perform this ritual in the natatorium." Ian raised his eyebrows and gave me a huge smile.

I nodded enthusiastically to Ian, for his use of such a sophisticated word. Ian looked at Meg and her face was blank. "It means swimming p..."

"I know what it means, dork," Meg snapped.

"Yeah right." Ian rolled his eyes.

Meg scowled.

"Should I proceed?" I inquired, hoping to break up the tension.

"Go for it Kyle!" Ian gave me the thumbs up.

With both feet in the water, I was ready to take the plunge.

"Wait!" shouted Ian. "I'll time you." Ian opened the appropriate app on his cell phone.

"Start the time now, Ian."

I dove into the cool, blue sea.

All trepidation melted away as I swam deeper and deeper. I was changing, minute scales spreading over my entire body. My webbed hands and feet propelled me through the water at a rapid pace. It was so natural.

Suddenly, my vision brightened, I could see through the dark water. It was amazing! Vibrant colored coral, fish and sea creatures swam all around me.

My hearing heightened. A high-pitched whistle seemed to be coming from right beside me, but I could see nothing. The sound came again, but much louder now.

It was time to take a breath, so I rapidly swam to the surface. When I broke through the blanket of water that had graciously held me in its arms, I saw Ian and Meg on shore. They yelled and pointed at something behind me. I focused my hearing.

"Shark! Shark!" They screamed.

I spun around and saw a fin sticking out of the water. It headed toward me at a rapid pace. Funny, I didn't feel or sense fear, only curiosity. I dived back under the water, in the direction of the fin.

Moments later, I emerged with a new friend. Ian and Meg's shark was, in fact, a dolphin. I called him my friend because something magical was happening between us. We understood each other. It wasn't through sounds, but thoughts, more like feelings that had meaning to them.

Images flashed through my mind of this friendly porpoise pushing me out of a virtual tornado of water. I respectfully pet him, knowing that he had saved my life only weeks before.

I beckoned my new friend to join me closer to the shore, so I could introduce him to my land-dwelling companions. Ian and Meg both sat on a rock awaiting our arrival.

"Whoa!" Ian exclaimed. "Cool fish."

"Mammal," corrected Meg. "Sharks are fish. Dolphins are mammals, but it's a common mistake."

"I knew that," insisted Ian.

I exited the water and joined Ian and Meg on the edge of the shore. We waved to our new friend.

"He is happy to have met both of you," I said.

"You can communicate?" Meg asked.

"Dude, you are Aquaman! But way cooler." Ian shouted.

I laughed. "Thanks, Ian."

The dolphin didn't seem to share in Ian's humor. He slapped the water frantically and motioned toward us with his head.

"What's its deal?" Ian said.

I closed my eyes to focus on the dolphin's thoughts. He seemed to be disturbed at something or someone behind us.

I opened my eyes.

"There is someone..."

"Someone is watching us from the cliff." Meg got the words out before I could. Without warning, the dolphin swam away.

"Hey, where is it goin'?" Ian said disappointed.

"Not sure."

We all turned in unison toward the cliff behind us. There was a small flash of light.

"Hey," Ian yelled. "Someone snapped our picture."

"Listen," Meg said.

There was an engine roar, and the sound of tires spinning out on gravel. I couldn't quite distinguish the type of vehicle.

"It could be a ..."

"Motorcycle!" Ian and Meg shouted in unison. "Brad!"

We all ran toward the cliff, but only managed to get a few yards before we halted in our tracks.

"I think we are in trouble," Meg said with a quiver in her voice.

"Kyle! Kyle!" a shouting voice grew louder. Mary ran toward us with Roger in tow.

Anxiety flooded over me. Mary, Roger, and I had an unspoken agreement that I would not venture into the water without their permission and their presence.

Mary's approach was resonant with sadness and anger; she would have called the latter frustration. I wasn't sure which of these emotions was dominate, but I was about to find out.

Chapter 54
Wicked Chest Pass

You promised!" Mary screamed a foot in front of me. She didn't need to yell. I could hear her loud and clear.

"We trusted you, Jeremy." Mary grabbed me by the shoulder and shook me. "Why? How could you do this to us?"

"I'm so sorry, I..."

Mary struck me across the cheek.

"No, Jeremy! Stop it!"

Tears ran down my cheeks.

Mary took a step back.

"Kyle, I am so..." Mary collapsed onto the sand.

Roger rushed to her side, and cradled her in his arms. He looked up at me with tear-filled eyes. My heart ached; Ian and Meg were both sobbing too. In this small town, everyone knew the story of Roger and Mary's son's tragic death.

That was the longest and loneliest night I had in the lighthouse. I tossed and turned all night. My head and heart pounded with pain. The rain and wind slammed against my window. When I closed my eyes, all I saw was Mary in tears. I had all but forgotten about the possibility that Brad, my arch enemy, as Ian would say, may have seen my transformation, or at least seen us interacting with the dolphin.

How could I have been so thoughtless and selfish?
These were the people who loved me unconditionally, put my needs above their own, and made me feel special.

It may have been my imagination, but I thought I could still hear Mary crying, long into the night. I wondered what Ian and Meg were doing. Were they awake like me? Did they also view my actions as selfish? How could I fix this?

I got up before the sun. Quietly I prepared breakfast for Mary and Roger. Fresh orange juice, wheat toast, scrambled eggs and pancakes with real maple syrup; all of their favorites.

I even picked some fresh flowers from the garden. I put half the flowers in a vase on the table and the other half of the bouquet. The bouquet, I was taking with me to school.

Hopefully, the note I left would help them realize how truly sorry I was.

The hallways of the school were pretty empty this early in the morning. It was sort of nice and peaceful. A squeaking noise accompanied by the sound of pounding caught my attention. I followed the sounds to the gym where a basketball practice was in full swing.

"Hey!" an obnoxious voice called out. It was Brad. Was there anything this guy couldn't do?

"Where you going with those daisies, freak?"

"They're Trilliums."

"Whatever, weirdo," Brad spit out.

Pow! Without warning Brad hit me square in the chest with his basketball. I stumbled backward, tripped, and hit the ground hard. The bouquet of flowers, I had intended to present to Amber as an acceptance to her invitation, spilled all over the shiny gym floor.

Brad stood over me laughing. Anger, sadness, and shame swirled through me all at the same time. Embarrassingly, I began to cry.

Brad leaned down and whispered, "Don't cry too hard, fish boy. Tears are salty, you know."

I tried to speak, but choked on my words. Brad stood up and sneered. "I'm gonna tell everyone about you and your freaky friends."

"Please," I begged, stretching my hand up toward this towering bully.

"Please what?" Brad retorted.

"Leave my friends alone."

Brad looked down at me with a strange intensity. I could tell he was formulating a plan.

"Okay, crybaby. I'll leave you and your little freak show alone."

Brad paused. I didn't know whether to smile or continue being afraid. "You just need to stay clear of my girl."

"Who?" I said.

"Amber! Smart mouth."

How could Amber still be Brad's girl, when she had made it clear she wanted nothing to do with him anymore? The relationship seemed very one-sided.

"But the dance," I said without thinking.

"Boo, hoo!" Brad mocked me. "Guess you're goin' solo."

Brad leaned over and got even closer to me this time. His perspiration dripped on my face. Yuck.

"We got a deal, mermaid?" Brad demanded.

I knew I had no other choice but to acquiesce to this bully's intimidation. I nodded, and then wiped my tears, and Brad's sweat off my face.

"Smart choice, freak. Now pick up your pansies and get outta my gym."

"Trill..."

Brad sneered and strutted away. What an angry young man, and he sure did like to use the word "freak".

I rolled to my knees, gathered the fallen flowers, and scrambled to my feet. I didn't look back at Brad and his buddies, but I could hear laughter echoing through the gym. I fled the gymnasium red faced, sore chested, scared and embarrassed.

The hallway in front of me seemed to be narrowing and the lockers on either side of me were reaching out grabbing at my clothing. The tiles under my feet turned to mud. I was running, but could not move.

"Please, let me be in my bed dreaming." Any nightmare would be better than this reality.

Chapter 55
Forgiveness

Wham! A classroom door opened in front of me. I ran, or rather fell, head first into it.

"I'm so sorry," is all I heard before everything faded to black. The amount of times I've faded to darkness can't be healthy.

I woke up in the nurse's office. A woman held my hand and stroking my forehead.

"How long have ..."

"Mary! I thought you were the school nurse."

Mary's eyes were moist again. This time I could tell they were tears of joy. "Oh, Kyle," Mary held my hand tight. "I am so sorry. Can you forgive me?"

I quickly sat up. "Forgive you? No, please forgive me."

Mary smiled and we embraced, for what seemed like an hour. No words were necessary. We could feel the love and concern we had for each other.

After our hug, I looked around the room.

"Where is Roger? Is he still upset with me?"

Mary hugged me again. "Oh no dear, he is in the hallway speaking with your confidants."

I smiled. Her accepting Ian and Meg into our "circle of trust," as Roger called it, was a huge relief. This time, I initiated the hug. I squeezed Mary tight and whispered a sincere, soft "Thank you." Just then the real school nurse walked in.

"You are all clear to return to class, Kyle," the nurse said with a perky smile.

"Thank you so much," I responded.

"Mrs. Starr," the nurse continued. "If you could just fill out this form for me."

"Of course," Mary said.

"And Kyle," the nurse said.

"Yes ma'am?"

"Please be careful when walking through the halls. Keep your eyes up."

"Sound council, ma'am. Thank you so much."

After Mary completed the necessary paperwork we bid the nurse farewell and joined Roger, Ian and Meg in the hallway. I immediately ran over to Roger and squeezed him tight.

"Ha," Roger bellowed. "You're a strong one."

"Thank you Roger, thank you."

"Hey," Ian shouted. "We're here too."

I turned around and embraced my friends.

"You're the best."

Something felt odd. There were too many bodies in our "circle of trust". I took a step back and looked at Ian, then Meg, and then some stranger.

"Uh," I said embarrassed.

"It's all good, dude," the stranger said. "I'm down with the whole group hug thing. Strength in numbers right?"

I took another step back and looked this unfamiliar individual up and down. Wait, he was wearing one of those "Math Rules" t-shirts.

"Who are you?" I inquired.

"Kyle," Mary prompted me to mind my manners.

"Excuse me," I corrected myself. "Whom do I have the pleasure of meeting?"

I extended my hand for the customary greeting. The stranger slapped my hand instead.

"Name's Reggie," he said with exuberance. "I'm in the Math Club with Lego."

I looked at Meg, and she produced an awkward half smile.

Chapter 56
A Suitor for Meg

Sorry about the floras." Reggie handed me a crumbled, pathetic bunch of wilted, broken, trodden on flowers.

"Oh," I said, hesitantly taking the flowers, then holding them limp to my side. One stem escaped and flopped to the floor.

"They looked, well, nice," Reggie said.

"Want 'em," I said half sarcastically.

"You bet! With a little T.L.C. you can make anything grow."

Reggie took the flowers, and then handed the battered bouquet to Meg, put one arm around her, and pulled her close to him.

Meg winced and attempted to pull away, but Reggie held her tight.

Ian snickered.

I looked to Ian for clarification.

"Lego Mego asked Reginald to the dance," Ian announced.

Mary clapped her hands. "Oh, how wonderful!"

"Is it?" Roger's playful response received a poke to his ribs from Mary.

"It is wonderful, Mr. Starr," Reggie confirmed.

"What? When? Why?" I couldn't help myself. Reggie presented himself as intelligent enough for Meg, but he just didn't seem her type.

"Kyle!" Mary's reprove was sharper this time. Roger just chuckled. Mary gave him one of her "that's quite enough, dear" glares. Roger comically mimed zipping his mouth closed. I laughed, but quickly retracted before I also received one of Mary's glares.

"I know, I know," Reggie interjected. "What is an absolutely gorgeous girl like Ms. McGreggor doing going out with a guy like me?"

I cleared my throat. I wanted to say, "Exactly, what is Meg going out with you for?" but I could see Mary with my peripheral vision. Her impending glare told me to bite my tongue. Roger had taught me the rule of three strikes and you're out. Out to where I wasn't sure, but I certainly didn't want to incur Mary's wrath and find out.

"So, this happened when?" I inquired, trying to be polite and sincere.

"About an hour ago," Reggie replied.

"Wha...wonderful," I was glad to have caught myself, because now Mary's arms were folded in front of her, and Roger said that meant "she's a gettin' serious."

Reggie continued, undaunted by my stammering. "I actually have you to thank, Kyle."

"This should be good," Roger muttered.

Ian snickered and Meg took a breath before rolling her eyes.

"How so, dear?" Mary encouraged.

"Well," Reggie went on. "It was my door Kyle walked into. I mean, I opened the door and *bam*, next thing I know I'm looking down at a dead fish."

There was a very awkward silence, until Ian mumbled under his breath, "Mammal."

"What now?" Reggie addressed Ian.

"Who?" Ian responded.

"What?" Reggie insisted.

"That's when he called me," Meg interjected.

"He has your number?" I said with some shock.

"Well, I texted you first, but then I called."

"Yeah, then Meg called me," Ian said with pride.

"You twitched a little, so I thought it'd be safe if we all dragged you to the nurse's office. It was just around the corner," Reggie explained by pointing in the direction of the nurse's office.

"I took your feet," Ian gleefully announced.

I gulped with embarrassment and looked down at the floor. The thought of me being dragged like a sack of potatoes through the school hallway was causing my stomach to churn with shame.

"That was very kind of all of you. Perhaps next time calling for an adult would be appropriate." Mary's words were kind, yet gently reproving.

"Yes, ma'am," Ian said.

"Sorry, Mrs. Starr," Reggie added.

"Thank you, Reginald. I know all of you were just doing what you felt was right."

Reginald? Obviously, Mary was acquainted with this young man. Reggie must have known Mary well, and respected her, because he didn't correct Mary when she used what I assume was his proper name. Ian, of course, snickered. Before any reprimanding looks could be cast his way, he was saved by the bell, literally.

Reggie announced that he and Meg must leave for their next class. They had a class together? Why wasn't I notified?

I watched Meg and her new suitor walk down the hallway together, with my once proud and colorful bouquet of Trilliums. Reggie draped his arm around Meg leaned away and hunched her shoulders. I could tell she was visibly uncomfortable; at least that's what I chose to see.

"Such a nice young man," Mary commented, watching them disappear into a classroom.

"Is he?" Roger's inquiry seemed sincere.

"You remember Reginald dear," Mary paused, but Roger did not respond. "He helped you change a flat tire last spring."

Roger scratched his chin. "Wasn't he a lot shorter?"

"Good one Mr. Starr." Ian chuckled.

Roger gave Ian a look that said, "that wasn't supposed to be a joke."

Ian gulped. "I, uh, we better get to class too." Ian patted my shoulder. " Right, Kyle?"

I looked at the ground, and kicked my foot across the tile floor. "I guess."

Roger squeezed my shoulder. "The girl of your dreams asked you to the hop, and you are feeling glum?"

"What?" I said, surprised.

Mary squeezed my hand. "Mr. Kennedy told us the good news."

I gave Ian a not so friendly glare. His eyes widened and he took a step back.

"Kyle?" Mary gave me a puzzled look. "Don't be upset, your friend was just so excited to tell us. Sorry we didn't hear it from you first."

"Yeah," Roger added. "I thought you'd be burstin' to share the good news."

"Yeah, Kyle," Ian was attempting to redeem himself. "Why didn't you share?"

"Because I'm not going! That's why!" I adamantly said.

Ian, Roger, and Mary all looked at me in shock. They seemed to be frozen in time, each with their mouth gaping wide in disbelief.

Chapter 57
Rejection Rejected

I flung my backpack over my shoulder and started walking down the hallway.

"Wait up dude," Ian shouted, running after me.

"Whoa," Roger said. "Hold on, just a minute fellas."

Ian and I turned around. Roger and Mary walked toward us. Both had furled brows.

"Uh oh," Ian muttered. I just gulped.

Stopping in front of us, Roger put his hands on his hips and cocked his head to one side. Mary gently touched my cheek.

"We are just concerned about you." Mary said.

"Kid, you just got conked on the head by a door!" Roger added.

"I know, I know, but I feel fine. Right, Ian?"

Ian blinked and twitched his body a little. "What? Why you asking me?" Ian looked at Mary and Roger. "I mean he looks good and all."

"I'm too not sure about that," Roger said.

"Please, I really feel better," I said.

Roger and Mary exchanged glances. "If you promise to call us the minute you feel sick."

"I won't," I said.

Mary and Roger raised their eyebrows.

"I mean I won't feel sick."

After, what I was sure was an unsatisfactory goodbye to Mary and Roger, Ian and I shuffled briskly down the hallway to our next classes.

"Sorry, dude," Ian said before sliding into his class.

The classroom door closed behind him before I had a chance to respond. *Sorry for what*? Humiliatingly dragging me half-conscious through the school, to the nurse's office? Blabbing to the Starrs about Amber inviting me to the MOPR dance? Or allowing Meg to go out with that, that, dork?

Whoa! Mary would not have approved of such derogatory name calling. Even though I had not audibly expressed my thoughts, I still instinctively looked around to ensure that I wasn't overheard, especially by Mary.

Why was I allowing myself to become so upset over Meg being asked out? Who cared? She could do what whatever she wanted. I had bigger issues to deal with, like explaining to Amber I would not be accompanying her to the coveted social function.

I wouldn't see Ian or Meg again until lunch, and I knew they, with the best of intentions, would attempt to persuade me not to cancel my date with Amber.

Date with Amber; just thinking those words caused my heart to swell. I shook my head vigorously. I needed to push aside that thought. I was doing this to protect not only myself, but Mary, Roger, Ian and Meg. If Brad really had evidence of my aquatic transformation, then I had no choice but to decline Amber's sweet, creative, thoughtful, and very energetic invitation.

SLAP! I struck myself across the face. "Get your head together," I muttered. Just then I realized I was sitting in the middle of my geography class. All eyes were on me. I sunk down in my seat, and looked at my desk top.

"Something you'd like to share with the class Mr. Starr?" Mr. Yearsley, my geography teacher, asked in a sharp tone.

I gulped and felt instantly sick to my stomach. I had never been publicly reprimanded by a teacher before. I hoped my conduct did not get reported back to Mary.

So far, this school day was turning out to be one of the worst days ever.

When class finally ended, it was time to face the music. I needed to find Amber before her next class. If I waited much longer, I would run into my friends, and I knew "best intentioned" Ian, and maybe even Meg, would attempt to convince me not to go through with declining Amber's invitation.

I was feeling very weak and vulnerable, so I just might allow myself to be talked out of my intended action.

After turning a few corners, I came to the hallway where Amber's locker resided. I immediately froze. Brad walked straight toward me. My knees shook. I was frightened enough with the thought of having to face Amber, but now Brad had to show up too.

"Make it quick thalassic," Brad commanded, strutting toward me.

"What?" I thought. I didn't know whether to be taken aback by his arrogance, assuming I had come to decline Amber's invitation due to his intimidation tactics, or the fact that Brad used such a word outside his vocabulary range.

In a fraction of a second, my mind opened up various files of stored knowledge and information until I found the word "thalassic." Thalassic: adjective, growing, living or found in the sea. *Hmmm, I am impressed, Brad.*

"Yes, I wi..."

SMACK! Brad slammed into my shoulder. "Yeah, I know how to read the dictionary, dude." He laughed to himself and pompously strolled away.

I rubbed my shoulder and winched. *Is this all because of Amber? Wow, he must really, really be fond of her, or really, really dislike me.*

And there she was, the beautiful Amber, turning the combination of her locker. I gulped hard and steadied my nerves. Clearing my throat, I approach her with caution.

"Hello, Amber," my voice cracked. "I need to..."

"No." Amber turned and faced me.

"No?" I said.

"That's right, Kyle. I said no to your no."

I scratched my head. "Sorry, I'm a bit confused."

"No, you're not," Amber insisted. "You know perfectly well what I am talking about."

"That's a lot of no's," I said, hoping my attempt at humor would ease the tension. At least the tension I was feeling. It didn't work.

Amber looked at me, waiting for a sensible response. I looked back at her, hoping she would speak first, but she didn't.

"Huh, well..." I paused, wishing she would cut me off again. No such luck. Beads of perspiration formed on my forehead. I needed to say something, anything, but what? Her beautiful eyes were piercing my soul.

"What should I wear to the dance?" What? What was I saying? Wear to the dance? Had I lost all rational thought?

"I'll let Mrs. Starr know," Amber said in the sweetest, softest voice. "I have a feeling she'd love to help pick out your attire." Amber winked at me. She squeezed my hand, closed her locker and walked away.

I was mesmerized watching her walk down the hallway and out of sight. Then reality struck. I was going to get destroyed. Brad was going to pummel me, or worse, hurt my friends. I fell back against the lockers and sunk to the ground.

Lost in the image of being beaten by Brad, I didn't notice Ian, Meg and her new beau, Reggie, standing over me. Sounds were muffled, but I could tell they were asking me something. Finally, my head cleared, and their words became audible.

"Are you coming to lunch or not?" Ian asked. From the frustration in his voice, I think he'd asked me that question multiple times.

"You don't want us to carry you again, do ya?" Reggie laughed.

I made an effort to produce an insincere smile, but my face was too numb to create any such display. "I...I am feeling out of sorts."

Reggie laughed. "What? Who talks like this?" Reggie playfully bumped his shoulder into Meg's. "You're right Lego, he is unique and special."

I took Reggie's words as a compliment, especially if he was quoting Meg.

"Come on." Meg grabbed my forearm to pull me up.

"Yay." Ian joined in and grabbed my other arm. They both pulled with great force, but only managed to slump me forward. Then Reggie reached down. He was about to grab me around the waist.

"Okay," I said, jumping to my feet. "I'm up."

Chapter 58
No Room for Jell-O

Why did I agree to join this trio for lunch? I was practically painting a bullseye on my chest, head, and stomach; or wherever Brad was going to hit me next.

There was no escaping the inevitable now. I was just hoping Brad wouldn't, as Ian's said, "lay a beat down" on me here in the cafeteria.

"Earth to Kyle," Ian interrupted my fearful thoughts.

I realized I had "spaced out" again, another Ian phrase. At least this time I wasn't being embarrassed by a teacher in a classroom full of my peers.

Apparently I had been staring down at my uneaten baloney sandwich for quite some time.

I don't even remember taking the sandwich out of my lunch sack, let alone removing it from the confining plastic wrap. Baloney sandwich, I hated baloney. Of course, I couldn't tell Mary that, I didn't want to hurt her feelings.

Why couldn't I stand up for myself and speak my mind? Oh yeah, I attempted that once and it was a disaster. With all the knowledge and vocabulary words floating round in my head, one would think I would be better at expressing my honest feelings.

"Krypton to Kyle," Ian interrupted once again.

"What?" I replied.

"Earth wasn't working," Ian explained.

I forced a faux smile.

"Here," Ian pushed his cup of green Jell-O toward me. "This will perk you up." Ian peeled back the top of the container that held the bright, jiggling gelatin.

"You love this stuff!"

"No, thank you Ian."

"What!" Ian shook his head and sat back.

It was true, I did love that wiggly treat.

"Sorry, I'm just..."

"You're really wigged out there, dude," Reggie added. "You must have hit that door pretty hard."

I found the sound of Reggie's voice irritating.

"The term is spaced out, not wigged out!"

My voice rose so loud I drew the attention of the students who were sitting at nearby tables.

"And I didn't hit the door. The door hit me, thanks to you." I grit my teeth and returned to staring at my baloney sandwich.

Meg cleared her throat. "Reggie said it was an accident, Kyle. We are all friends here. Aren't we?"

Once again, I was experiencing yet a moment of shame and embarrassment. I wished I was home in my rocket ship pajamas, and tucked under my warm covers; perhaps with some of Roger's homemade cocoa on my night stand.

But the reality was that I was here, in the cafeteria, and I had inadvertently hurt my dear friend, Meg. I hung my head even lower and mumbled, "Sorry."

"It's okay, Kyle." Meg softly said.

I looked up, and was met by Meg's kind, forgiving eyes. Then I started to tremble and beads of perspiration formed on my forehead and nose. I gulped hard, and returned my gaze to the top of the lunch table.

"Bro, you look like you're about to barf. Meg said everything is cool." Reggie pronounced.

Reggie's concern for my seemingly erratic behavior was understandable. However, it was not Meg causing my distress.

I slowly raised my hand and pointed over Meg's shoulder. Ian sat up a little higher in his seat so he could peer over Meg. Both Meg and Reggie turned around to see what I was pointing at.

There he was, my nemesis, grinding his tightly clenched fist. There was no escaping; Brad was going to pummel me for not declining Amber's invitation to the dance. Nausea accompanied by perspiration and trembling overcame me.

"Uh," Reggie's voice squeaked. "He is coming over here."

I froze.

Run Kyle.

Why was I not running? I was literally immobile. Fear gripped me tight and wouldn't let go. Ian looked as sick as I felt. He took a huge gulp, and in a shaky voice said, "I got your back, bro."

Chapter 59
Meg Goes Toe to Toe

Ian began to stand up when Meg reached across the table. Placing her hand on top of mine, she said, "I'll take care of this."

Before I could speak, Meg stood up, turned around, and faced the approaching bully. Brad stopped a few feet away from Meg.

"What?" Brad snapped at Meg.

"Exactly," Meg said. "What do you got?"

"Huh?" Brad responded.

"Nice bluff, Brad, but it won't work."

"What are you talkin' about?" Brad now seemed more irritated than angry.

Meg looked back at me and winked. Reggie just stared at the tabletop. Some brave boyfriend he was; I guess Ian and I weren't much better though. Brave I mean, not boyfriends. I guess I should have said something, but Meg was confidently in control of the situation.

"What were you snapping pictures with the other night, Brad?" There was an awkward pause. "Your cell phone." Meg's question caused Brad to pause.

"Well," Meg continued.

"That's right detective," Brad said sarcastically. "And I'm gonna post 'em all online, if gill boy don't do as he's told."

I looked at Reggie, worried that Brad's comment was going to raise suspension, but Reggie didn't flinch. I wasn't sure he was even conscious. His eyes were still fixed on the top of the table. He wasn't even blinking.

Ian nudged me, and I returned my gaze to Meg and Brad. Brad waved his cell phone in Meg's face.

"Is that supposed to convince me?" Meg said.

"I'll blast these all over the internet!" Brad's voice grew in intensity, but it wasn't convincing.

"Go ahead," Meg wasn't backing down. "I'm surprised you can even use a computer."

Brad growled and took a step toward Meg. She stood perfectly still. Ian and I stood up in unison. We looked at each other, both a bit surprised in our courageous action.

"Your grandma's flip phone!" Meg continued to discredit Brad. "At night! You were at least a hundred feet away."

Meg turned to us and smiled. We nodded affirmatively. "You got nothing Brad."

Not even waiting for his response, Meg returned to our table and sat back down beside an unresponsive Reggie. Ian and I exchanged an awkward look before simultaneously sitting down.

Brad's mouth dropped open, but nothing came out. After a few moments of standing alone, Brad's face became red and his eyes welled up. We ignored him and began trading lunch items. Brad took a few steps backward before turning around and stomping out of the cafeteria.

"Phew," Reggie wiped his brow. "That was a close one."

Meg rolled her eyes and Ian snickered. I was awe struck. Meg was amazing. Her courage, her poise, her tenacity; I could not help but stare at her, not in a creepy way, but in adoration.

Meg looked up from rifling through her lunch sack and caught me gawking at her. Funny, I didn't look away; I simply gave Meg a smile of appreciation. Meg tilted her head and her soft hair fell to one side. She squinted at me, and then returned a genuine smile. At that moment, I knew Meg and I were forging a friendship that would last forever.

Chapter 60
Gettin' the Groove On

Days had past, and there was no retaliation from Brad. In fact, I didn't recall seeing him around school at all. I guess Meg really shook some sense into him. So, I should have been feeling pretty calm, right? No, now I have a whole different reason for being nervous... I couldn't dance.

"No problem," Ian said. "I got you covered, dude."

Ian had volunteered to come over after school and teach me some of his "signature moves."

On the walk up the driveway, Ian bombarded me with a barrage of questions.

"Never?" Ian asked. "Not even once?"

"Not that I can remember," I answered.

"But you've seen it before, right?"

"No, I can't say I have." I admitted.

"Not even your parents?"

I hung my head and kicked a small rock that lay on the dirt driveway.

"Sorry, dude," Ian said. "I forgot that you forgot, I mean can't remember."

"No worries," I said.

I knew Ian meant well. I was just hoping with the big event being only two days away Ian could work his magic without all the inquiries.

"How was school today, fellas?" Roger said, walking out of the garage.

"Uneventful," I replied.

"What you doin', Mr. Starr?" Ian asked.

Roger looked down at the metal pan in his hands, and then back at Ian. "Changing my oil."

"Are you not feeling well?" I asked.

There was silence. Ian grimaced and Roger just looked at me dumbfounded. After a moment, I produced a sly grin. Roger broke out into a chuckle, and Ian slapped me on the back.

"Nice one Kyle," Ian bellowed. "Isn't he the best?"

"He certainly is," Roger nodded.

Once in the house, we received permission from Mary to move the family room furniture around, in order to clear an area large enough for me to practice.

Mary leaned up against the doorframe behind us. Her arms were folded, and she was holding a dish towel. I looked over my shoulder and gritted my teeth in an attempt to convey what she was about to witness could be very embarrassing for all of us.

"Shall I leave?" Mary whispered.

I was about to say please, when Ian chimed in. "Not at all," Ian said. "My moves are for public consumption."

Mary put her hand over her mouth, politely covering up her giggle.

Ian set his "boom box" on the counter and inserted a small round disc.

"My folks still use vinyl, Mrs. Starr," Ian said. Mary nodded with approval. "Me, I'm trying to keep CDs alive."

"Very admirable, Ian," Mary complimented.

Ian pressed a button and some rhythmic music came forth. Ian waved me to the center of the floor.

"You ain't gonna learn anything staying over there Kyle." Roger had poked his head around Mary's shoulder. "Dance lessons huh?" Roger inquired.

"Yep," Ian said while gyrating his body around the open family room floor. "Turns out that super Kyle can't dance."

I gulped hard.

"Or, at least he forgot how," Ian added.

"Well, best give`er a go then," Roger said addressing me.

I took a tentative step to the center of the room. With fear in my eyes, I looked back a Roger and Mary for encouragement. Mary gave me a nod and Roger winked. What happened next can only be described as a complete disaster. Not with regards to Ian's movements, he was quite good as far as I could tell.

After a series of hip twists, splits and something he called the "moonwalk," Mary and Roger broke out in sincere applause. Then it was my turn.

Chapter 61
Two Left Feet

My first move was an Elvis hip thrust. I heard and audible "eww" from Ian. Next I attempted what Ian had described as "The Running Man". I slipped on the family room rug. It slid out from under me and I crashed down on both knees.

Since I was already close to the ground, I attempted the splits, but unlike Ian, the only thing I split was my pants. I thought everyone would have been laughing at me by now, but I think they were too horrified.

Finally, since I wanted to end with a bang, I went into the "Michael Jackson" spin. How was Ian able to keep his balance? My whirl wind turned into a tornado of destruction. Spinning out of control, I crashed into the end table, sending myself and a lamp smashing to the floor.

"Oh, my word." Mary rushed to assist me.

"You okay, bro?" Ian inquired.

Roger put the end table and lamp back in place.

"Nothing broke here," Roger said. "How 'bout you Kyle, anything hurt?"

I stood up, rubbed my head, and my posterior. "Just my pride, sir."

Everyone chuckled, even me.

"Have a seat on the couch boys," Roger admonished. "It's my turn to show you a thing or two."

Ian and I did as we were told. We sat on the couch, in anticipation. Ian gave me a pat on the shoulder. "Nice attempt Kyle. With a little practice you'll be Kevin Bacon in no time."

"Who?" I said.

Ian gasped. He covered his mouth with one hand, slowly shaking his head at me. "You have a lot to learn my young padawan."

Roger turned off Ian's music and went over to the record player. He carefully perused his collection of albums until he found what he was looking for. The large square envelope had a picture of a man on the cover named Nate King Cole. Another King, this was going to be good.

"Nice tunes, Mr. S," Ian said, giving Mary a smile and nod. Mary smiled back.

The music began to play, and it was intoxicating. What a smooth, deep, rich voice. Ian and I swayed back and forth, in time with the music.

"Now this is soul," Ian said with exuberance.

Roger motioned for Mary to join him on the makeshift dance floor. "Boys," Roger had our attention. "If you really wish to woo your ladies, you best learn to slow dance."

Ian looked at me and shrugged. I wasn't any the wiser either. Mary joined Roger, and they glided across the family room floor. Wow, this was art in motion. Roger was a man of hidden talents.

As they continued with a variance of dances from one song to another, I imagined Amber and me dancing together, swaying back and forth across the High School gym dance floor. I sighed in anticipation of the moment.

"They are really good," Ian said out of the corner of his mouth.

Snapped out of my day dream, I watched Roger and Mary with more of a concentrated effort. It wasn't only their dancing that was captivating; it was the expression of pure love each had on their face. For some reason, I could easily identify that emotion when it is being expressed. The twinkle in their eyes, the subtle smile on their faces, and the glow of their skin were all indicators that I was witnessing true love in motion.

The last song on the record concluded, and Roger and Mary took a bow. I immediately stood and clapped. Ian pushed himself up from the couch and joined me.

"That was exquisite!" I clapped with more vigor.

"Last time I saw dancin' like that, I was at my cousin's wedding," Ian added.

Roger glanced at Mary, and raised his eyebrows.

"We'll take that as a compliment," Mary said.

Ian gulped. "Oh, I meant it as one, really." Ian adjusted his glasses. "It's just...how are me and Kyle supposed to learn how to dance like that?"

Mary and Roger looked at each other, then at us. "Practice," they said in unison.

Chapter 62
Dancing with the Starrs

Before we knew it, Ian and I were dancing in the middle of the living room, with each other!

Roger and Mary danced beside us, giving us step by step instructions, on where to place our hands and feet. It was incredibly awkward, to say the least.

"This is too weird," Ian said, for the third time.

"You are doing very well following my lead," I said, with a slight smirk.

"Thank you," Ian paused for a moment. "Wait. What?" Ian was indignant. "I'm not the girl." Ian looked at Roger and Mary, who were already chuckling. "Am I supposed to be the girl?"

Roger and Mary nodded. Ian looked at me, and I gave him a wink. "Eww." Ian immediately released his hand hold and took a step back.

"Why don't we change partners?"

"Mr. Kennedy," Mary curtsied to Ian. "Will you do me the honor?"

Ian quickly took Mary in a lead hold position. "It'd be my pleasure." Ian said. He looked at me and stuck out his lower lip. I laughed.

"May I have this dance?" Roger's deep voice added to the discomfort of the situation. Roger extended his hand toward me. I cringed.

"Ha!" Ian laughed. "We the men now. Right Mr. Starr?" Ian slapped Roger's extended hand.

"Mr. Kennedy," Mary gently chided. "You are out of hold."

"Sorry, ma'am," Ian apologized.

Roger gave Ian a pat on the shoulder. "Take good care of my lady now."

"Yes sir," Ian replied with renewed determination. "We can do this Kyle."

I wasn't so sure. I looked at Roger and gulped. He straightened up and looked off to the side with his head lifted in a blasé pose. It reminded me of some of the ladies in Mary's Jane Austen shows. Mary said the women were just acting coy, but really wanted the attention of the gentleman caller. It was both amusing and strange to see Roger performing this role; but I thought I better indulge him.

"It would be my greatest honor if you would grant me this dance, miss," I said to Roger in my best British accent. Mary giggled. Roger let out a bellow.

"Ha! We got ourselves two right young gentlemen here Mary."

"Two of the best," Mary added.

"Take the lead, Kyle," Roger insisted.

This was almost worse than dancing with Ian. At least Ian's hands were soft. Roger's hands were rough and worn, from years and years of hard work. Despite the fact that Roger was much taller than me, I think I did pretty well.

After a few songs, I asked if I could dance with Mary, since we were concluding our lessons. Roger acquiesced to my request. No fair I thought, watching Ian and Roger take a time on the couch, as Mary and I glided around the room. Ian didn't get the pleasure of dancing with Roger like I had.

"You two going to join us?" Mary asked.

Roger slapped his knees. "Don't mind if we do, sweetheart." Roger pulled Ian up, much to his dismay, and they both joined Mary and me in our dance position. All four of us joined hands and swayed back and forth in a circle.

"I think the lads are ready, honey," Roger said, winking at me and Ian.

"Thanks for the training," I said.

"Yeah," Ian added. "A little weird, but fun. Thanks."

"You are both very welcome," Mary said. "I think you two are ready for the real dance floor. Your young ladies will be very impressed."

Ian looked at me and gave a big, cheesy grin. "Now all we need are some awesome suits."

Chapter 63
Dressed to Dance

Can you believe it's tonight?" Ian said, with unbridled enthusiasm. He was grinning so hard I thought his cheeks were going to explode.

"Yeah, it really is," I said with trepidation.

"Relax Kyle," Ian reassured me. "You'll feel much better when we get you into some cool threads."

"Are you sure we are going to find what we are looking for in here?"

"Of course," Ian replied. "Look at this sweet one." Ian held up a neon yellow suit jacket. We were standing in the middle of a local thrift store. Ian said our dollars would really stretch here. Ironically, the store was called "Dollar Stretch."

"What do you think of this one?"

Ian held up a neon pink suit, covered in a pattern of small yellow daisies.

"Bright," I said.

"It's incredible, it's awesome." Ian paused, and then snickered.

"I am gathering that was a line from a movie, or a comic book."

"It's from Napoleon Dynamite!"

"Who?" I said.

Ian shook his head. "You got a lot of culture to learn my friend."

I smiled, and returned to looking at the various racks of clothing in the thrift store. "You know Mary wasn't very happy when I came here before. I don't think she will approve any of my choices." I held up a bright green three-piece suit.

"Oh, that's nice," Ian said. "But I think red is more your color."

Ian searched through a few suits until he found a brilliant, red one. The pant legs had a shiny, silver stripe down each of the sides. "Yeah, this is definitely the one." Ian beamed with pride.

"I don't know what Amber will think."

"Dude, she'll love it." Ian was confident. "Trust me, Kyle."

"Okay, dude. I will." I mimicked Ian's tonality.

"Ha!" Ian let out a loud laugh. "It sounds so funny when you say it."

"What?"

"Duuude," Ian snickered.

"You are correct, Ian." I smiled. "It does sound humorous when I say it."

Ian tossed both the suits into our shopping cart. "Now let's find some vintage kicks, and some puffy shirts."

"Kicks?" I said.

"Yeah, you know," Ian paused waiting for me to catch on.

I didn't.

"Sneakers?"

I still looked at him with a blank stare. Ian sighed. "Tennis shoes, runners," Ian pointed down at my feet. "Those things, with the laces."

"Oh," I said. "My comfies."

"What?"

"My comf..."

"No, I heard you, Kyle. Why would call them that?"

I shuffled my feet, now feeling a little embarrassed.

"Well?" Ian persisted.

I cleared my throat and gave what I hoped was a dignified explanation. "When Mary took me clothes shopping, she said, *'Make sure you choose something very comfortable and cozy for your feet, your feet can regulate how your entire body feels.'*

Ian stared at me in awe. His mouth was wide open, and his eyes glazed over. I didn't think I'd ever seen him speechless.

I swallowed hard. "I suppose I could have called them my cozies?"

Ian blinked several times before bending over and laughing. I looked around the store to find several customers gazing in our direction. I sheepishly bent down to hide behind some racks of clothing. My efforts were futile; at the end of our row stood a group of girls, much younger than us, shook their heads while Ian continued to chortle. I grimaced and tapped Ian on the shoulder.

"Um... Ian?" I said. "Let's go find the foot wear you're talking about."

Ian managed to control his laughter enough to nod his head. We tried to inconspicuously exit the suit section.

Thankfully, the foot wear department was on the other side of the store. After several failed attempts trying on shoes, Ian and I found matching shiny high tops.

Ian kept calling them our "magical, hip-hop kicks." Sometimes his vernacular was beyond my comprehension.

In jest, I asked if I could call them my "sparklies." This time my comment did not elicit any outrageous laughter, just a scrunched expression and a head shake of disappointment. Obviously, my comic timing needed some work.

Our shopping excursion concluded. Ian and I were now headed back to his place. As we walked, Ian inquired about corsages. I explained that, Mary was going to provide the corsages Ian and I would adorn our dates with. Mary has quite the green thumb. Yes, that term was explained to me by her and Roger. I knew it must be some sort of metaphor when I first heard it.

"Okay," Ian said. "You want me, my mom, and McKenzie to pick you up around 5:30pm?"

"Well..." I started to say.

"You're right," Ian continued. "Better make it 5:00pm, that way we'll beat the dinner crowd."

"Actually, Mary and Roger have invited Amber and me to ride with them to the dance."

Ian cocked his head, and gave me a puzzled look.

"What do mean, invited you to ride with them?"

"Well, Roger and Mary are coming too."

"What?" Ian shouted.

Chapter 64
Adult Supervision

They said since they're both alumni, an invitation had been extended to them to... hmmm, what's the word," I paused for a moment and allowed my mind to recall the conversation I had with the Starrs. "Oh yes," I said, feeling very pleased with myself, "chapearo."

"You mean chaperone!" Ian was still shouting.

I was a little embarrassed having mispronounced the word, so I simply smiled and nodded.

"Argh," Ian slapped his forehead. "No offense, Kyle, but that is a definite buzz kill."

"Sounds violent," I said.

Ian shook his head. "Kyle, Kyle, sometimes, actually, most of the time." Ian put his arm around me. "With Ma and Pa looking on it's going to be pretty awkward getting any romance on."

"Romance on?"

"Yeah, you know," Ian looked around and then spoke in whisper. "Hand holding and dancing cheek to cheek."

"Oh!" I smiled with delight at the thought of holding onto Amber's hand, for an extended period of time. I became lost in my thoughts, and began to sway back and forth.

"Oh brother," Ian said, rolling his eyes.

Ian's remark did not deter me. I began daydreaming of holding Amber's silky, soft hands. I reflected on the day we met outside the clothing store; it was the first time our hands met. I was filled with bliss then, and I was still filled with bliss now. The anticipation of putting my hand is hers caused my heart to pound.

Ouch! My revelry was rudely interrupted by a sharp poke to my shoulder.

"Why Ian, why?"

"Dude, come back to earth."

"Sorry," I blinked in an attempt to focus. "I was just daydream..."

"I know, I know, but we need to pick up the pace. I told my mom I'd be home in time for a fresh haircut."

Ian ran his fingers through his shaggy, blonde hair. "I think I might go old school."

"Old school?" I questioned.

"Yeah, maybe a little Kevin Bacon."

This time I was familiar with Ian's reference. Before our afterschool shopping adventure, we stopped by Ian's residence. He showed me his video compilation of his favorite dance sequences from the cinema.

We watched scenes from Footloose, Beat Street, Breakin' 2: Electric Boogaloo, a little unsettling I must say, and one Mary would even approve of, Singing in the Rain.

I was surprised Ian used clips from the latter, but he said Gene Kelly made dance tough and cool for dudes. Also, Ian's mom was a big fan.

My mind went back to the image of holding Amber's hand. "Do you really think the Starrs' presence at our social function will mitigate our opportunity for sweet romance?"

Ian turned his head slowly and gave me his dead eyed stare. "Yes Kyle," Ian spoke at a slow and exaggerated pace, enunciating his words. "I do believe having Mary and Roger attend the dance is gonna mitigate our chances for romance."

Chapter 65
Road to Romance

This is so exciting!" I bounced up and down on the back seat of Mary's Buick. "I thought O'Blue was fun. No offense Roger, but this, this is like floating on water."

"Easily amused." Ian sat across from me, carefully holding the boutonniere Mary had created for his date, McKenzie. "And it's air, not water."

Roger chuckled and patted the dashboard. He was in the passenger seat. Mary loved to drive her Buick and referred to her car as "Bessie."

Apparently, inanimate automobiles received pet names. From what I discovered through the viewing of TV, Bessie was usually a name given to a bovine.

"Take a left up here, Mrs. Starr," Ian instructed.

Mary cleared her throat.

"Please," Ian added.

Mary smiled and gave Ian a wink via the rear-view mirror. Ian returned Mary's wink with a full toothed smile. Roger chuckled.

"It's the third house on the right." Ian's enthusiasm was boiling over. He vigorously bounced up and down on his seat. "There!" he shouted. "The green one!"

Mary's Buick slowed down. "I am looking forward to meeting McKenzie," I told Ian.

"Actually." Ian blushed a little. "It's Jolene."

"Who?" I said.

"Jolene," Ian continued. "From Math Lab."

"I thought that was McKenzie?"

Ian leaned toward me and whispered, "McKenzie is her name, but she goes by her middle name, Jolene."

"I don't get it," I said.

"Me neither," Ian replied. "Maybe it's cause I always called her MJ when we was kids."

I got the reference. Apparently, Roger did too, because I heard an audible snicker coming from the front seat. I looked up in time to see Roger covering his mouth. Out of the corner of her eye, Mary gave Roger the "now, behave yourself" look. The scene caused me to smile.

"Here, here!" Ian's high pitched voice of excitement resonated through the car.

This time both Roger and Mary chuckled

"Right here, Mr. Kennedy," Mary gently said.

"Yes please!" Ian exclaimed, as he bounded from the car. He was so enthusiastic with his exit that he left the car door open.

"Should I..."

"It's fine, Kyle," Roger anticipated my question. "I'm sure the young squire will return to us promptly."

Mary smiled at Roger's flowery words. She must have also squeezed his knee, because he made a gurgling, giggle sound. He only made it when Mary was tickling his knees.

Roger was correct. Young squire Ian returned promptly with a radiant, beautiful young lady holding onto his arm. Ian strutted down the pathway in his tuxedo full of confidence and giving his date the occasional wink and smile.

"Wow, Ian is just like Bruce Wayne."

Ian adjusted his bow tie and opened the car door for his lady friend. The attractive young lady slid into the car and sat beside me. Her sparkling dress matched Ian's shiny sneakers.

"Hi, Kyle," she said.

"Hi...um," I stuttered. Which name was I supposed to use? The pretty girl smiled at me; seemingly waiting for my response.

"What a beautiful dress, Jolene." Mary saved me from further embarrassment.

I gulped and tried again. "Most beautiful Jolene," I said with an exaggerated smile.

"Thank you, Kyle." Jolene blushed a little. "And you have a nice suit."

"Ian picked it out for me."

"You bet I did!" Ian proudly agreed.

"He does have good taste." Jolene smiled.

I nodded in agreement. "Sure does." Oops, that may have sounded inappropriate. It must have been, because when I turned, Ian gave me a scowl. I stared at him with a blank expression. After a pause, Ian laughed and punched me in the arm. I grimaced, and smiled back at Ian through clenched teeth.

"I believe we have arrived, young Kyle," Roger announced. His attempt to sound proper caused me to smile. When I looked at Amber's front door, my smile faded. I felt nausea, and I began to tremble.

"Breathe," Mary said, looking at me in her rearview mirror.

I nodded.

Ian buddy punched me in the shoulder. He really enjoyed doing that. "You got this, dude." Ian's enthusiasm was unrestrained. "You the man!"

Chapter 66
A Dream Walking

With teeth gritted, I swallowed hard, nodding rapidly. I certainly didn't feel like the man, but here I went anyway. The walkway to Amber's house seemed to stretch forever. I felt stares coming from the car. When I glanced over my shoulder, Mary, Roger, Ian and Jolene looked away from me.

Come on, Kyle, it's just a date. A date! This is really happening; I soon will be on the dance floor, holding hands with the most beautiful girl I have ever seen.

I looked down at my feet and realized I was already on Amber's front door mat. I took one more glance at the car. This time everyone, but Ian, was pretending to look away. Ian pressed up against the car window and gave me the two thumbs up. I raised my head in feigned confidence, and turned to ring the doorbell.

"May I help you, young man?" a sophisticated gentleman with streaks of black in his silver-gray hair said through the screen door.

"Good evening sir. Um, sorry, I didn't realize the inside door was open."

"It wasn't," the man said.

I gulped and we looked at each other in awkward silence.

"Might Amber be at home?" I squeaked out.

All I received was a blank stare. Well, maybe not so much a blank stare, more of an expression of disbelief.

"My name is Kyle Starr. I will be escorting Amber to this evening's dance."

I knew I had brushed my teeth, twice, used mouthwash, and even consumed the breath mint Ian offered me, when we initially got into the car. The way Amber's father winced, and turned away from me had me wondering if I had a bad case of halitosis.

"Sir, I..." He was gone before I could form a complete sentence.

Perplexed, I turned toward the car and shrugged.

Roger and Mary nodded in my direction, and Ian and Jolene pointed vigorously, instructing me to turn back toward the house.

Ian being the most enthusiastic of the pair looked almost frantic. I slowly turned my head and looked into the house. I looked through the open door, and there she was. Amber stood half-way down the flight of stairs.

"Beautiful," is all that came out of my mouth.

At least I think those were the words that came out of my gaping mouth. If not, I must have looked ridiculous, standing there frozen, with my "pie hole open so wide you could drive a tractor into it." Another one of Roger's clever quips.

Everything was in slow motion. Amber glided toward me in her shiny, teal dress. I was dreaming. I had to be. Amber reached the bottom of the stairs and placed my hand gently in hers. A pleasant shock streamed through my entire body, and my pulse raced.

Nope, I was wide awake, and reveling in every second of this blissful moment of joy.

"You look really handsome, Kyle."

Gulping hard I tried to speak, but nothing came out.

"Thank you is the appropriate response, Kyle." I could hear Mary's gentle voice in my head.

"Thank you, Amber," I said sincerely. "Allow me." I extended my arm and elbow toward Amber. Amber nodded and wrapped her hand around my bicep. Man, I wish I had done a few more push-ups in gym class today.

Amber smiled as we walked toward the car, so I guess my muscle tone wasn't too bad.

"11:45," came a rough voice from behind us. Amber and I turned to see her father standing on the porch with his arms crossed. I opened my mouth to speak, but Roger beat me to it.

"Will do, Doc!" Roger called from the car window.

Doctor Dawson produced a tiny smile in the right corner of his mouth, so I smiled at him, but I received his glare in return. His face was instantly stern again.

Amber squeezed my hand, and shook her head at her father. It might have been my imagination, but I think he winked at her before going back into the house.

"Come on." Amber pulled me toward the car.

Chapter 67
Trouble in Paradise

After a brief, bumpy ride; filled with nervous laughter, giggles, and a short embarrassing story from Roger about his lack of coordination during his first prom date with Mary, we finally arrived at the school. The exterior of the school looked pretty much the same, except it was night. But the interior was transformed into something magnificent.

Oval shaped colored balls suspended only by a thin cord dotted the whole gym ceiling. Shiny strands of material hung from the rafters. A cacophony of sounds pounded the walls of the gym, and flashing lights erupted in time with the beat of the music.

"Whoa!" All of us said in unison.

Wide-eyed we stood in the entranceway to the gym. Amazing, Beautiful, Wicked Cool were some of the terms we used to describe the cleverly decorated gymnasium in front of us.

"Let's go," Jolene said, grabbing Amber's hand. They took off into the crowd of already dancing young ladies.

"I'm game." Ian took a step forward, but I didn't move. I couldn't.

Swirls of color danced around a sunken marble castle. The castle shimmered in pure blue water. I was in awe watching a movie that suddenly started playing in my mind. I felt as if I were swimming toward the castle. My arms involuntarily twitched. Strokes brought me within feet of a beautifully crafted, ornate door.

The door opened of its own volition. I felt myself swim inside. Standing before me was a beautiful woman with long, flowing red hair. The woman was dressed in a metallic yellow gown. Her smile was kind and friendly. She motioned for me to join her.

Now I was walking, or rather floating toward this radiant woman; my feet did not touch the ground. Gliding closer my heart pounded with anticipation. Who was she? Why was I being summoned to her?

The pounding of my heart grew stronger. I felt like I was being hit in the chest. I grimaced in pain and the smile on the woman's face faded. The woman disappeared, and I felt another pound on my chest.

"No, come back!" I shouted.

I blinked and now saw Brad's clenched fist coming toward my chest. I grabbed his wrist and twisted his arm.

"Let go of me freak!" Brad yelled.

Brad's knees buckled, and I immediately let go.

"Pardon me, I…"

Brad didn't let me even get to the apology. "Shut your mouth! It's time to morph, you freak."

"Morph?" I was sure Brad was confused; but to avoid causing him any further disdain for me, I attempted a ginger approach.

"Hmm, I was positive our function tonight was called MORP. Of course, I could be mistaken."

"You're an idiot!"

"Brad." I shook my head in shame. "That is not very poli…"

A rough bump from behind cut me off. Within moments, I was surrounded by Brad, and what I gathered were three of his allies. I started to feel uncomfortable and nervous.

"Hello." My voice was loud and shaky. "You must be Brad's homies. Are you enjoying this evening activity?"

The three boys burst out laughing. I smiled, happy I could make them laugh. My goofy smile instantly dropped when my eyes met Brad's scowling face.

"Told you he was stupid."

I wanted to reprimand Brad for his rude comment, but I had the feeling I was in imminent danger.

Brad had his hands on his hips and snarled at me. The other three boys curiously had their hands behind their backs. Brad smirked before yelling, "Get 'im!"

Water filled balloons flew toward me. I should have used my powers to suspend the water balloons in midair, but instead used my hands to try and cover my face.

Splat! As soon as the balloons explored on me, I knew I was changing.

"No!" My shriek was loud and high pitched. More reasons to be embarrassed.

"Why are you worrying about the sound of your voice? You are in real trouble here Kyle!"

I collapsed to my knees, my hands over my face. I felt the salty water drip down my hands and the uncovered parts of my face. *Please let the dim lights in the gym conceal any transformation.*

Chapter 68
Kyle Unmasked

From the loud, maniacal laughter produced by Brad, I knew that my attempt to hide myself had failed.

How did Brad know to put salt in the water balloons? It's not as if the school's plumbing supplies salt water?

My eyes welled up with tears. *Keep it together Kyle. Don't add to your misery by balling.*

I slowly stood up and pulled my hands off my face.

"Look at the freak from the sea!" Brad shouted.

I turned my hands over and just and I feared, tiny blue and green scales speckled the back of each hand.

Brad's boys stared, each with mouth wide open.

It couldn't have only been my hands that caused their dumbfounded expressions. I reached up felt tiny scales on the sides of my face and neck, where the water hit.

A small ground gathered, and they too had their mouths wide open. Nobody moved, except Brad.

"Come you guys!" Brad shouted once again. "He's a freak!"

The three boys and some members of the crowd slowly looked at each other. A few even nodded in silence.

One of Brad's boys took a small step forward. His face went from a look of shock to a half smile.

"Grandpa's stories were true."

The music died down and lights came on. More students joined the curious crowd.

"Awesome!" came a high-pitched shout from the crowd.

"Totally awesome!" Ian pushed his way through the group of onlookers.

"Look ya'll, Red Rock High has it's very own Superhero!"

Ian looked at the students, then back at me.

"Yikes, tough crowd," he nervously said.

"We should leave," I recommended.

Ian nodded, "Yeah, let's bolt."

Brad stepped in front of us.

"You ain't goin' nowhere." He scowled at Ian and me.

We both produced simultaneous, audible gulps. The crowd began to murmur. I could hear various whispers. Kids were talking about me. "Is that a mask?" "Hey, move, I can't see." "Is he wearing makeup?" "Alien, he must be an alien."

Brad's homie, who had previously started to say something about his grandpa, approached me.

I waited for my beating, but it didn't come. Instead he cautiously put his hand on my shoulder. He looked me straight in my eyes. I couldn't believe it, there were tears in his eyes.

The boy gulped hard and spoke in a soft voice. "Grandpa wasn't going crazy."

I smiled at the boy, he smiled back.

Brad spun the boy around and shoved him to the floor.

"You're an idiot James!"

James just sat on the floor, a pleasant smile on his face. Brad made a fist, and motioned toward the fallen boy. James looked up at Brad and laughed. His laughter was accompanied by tears. It was very odd. Ian and I looked at each other, and then back at James. He grinned at both of us.

This could be our chance to escape. We turned to run.

"What is going on here?" The all too familiar voice of Principal Stern boomed across the dance floor.

Principal Stern pushed his way through the ever-growing crowd. "Mr. Edwards, what are you…"

"Arrest him!" Brad shouted, pointing at me.

Principal Stern stood motionless. Ian took a protective step in front of me and snarled at Brad. "Try it."

"You'll do no such thing!" Mary's commanding voice snapped Principle Stern out of his gaze.

"I…we, should, um…" Principal Stern stammered and blinked his eyes. Roger put his hand on Principal Stern's shoulder.

"It's okay Hank," Roger said in a calm voice. "The boy has a skin condition is all, an allergic reaction of sorts."

Roger's words didn't comfort Hank, I mean Mister, Principal Stern. He was visibly shaking.

"Where's Meg?" I inquired.

What? With Principle Stern in shock and the student body ready to send me off to the circus, I'm thinking about Meg?

Regardless, I surveyed the crowd looking for her, but I saw Amber instead. I felt a twinge of disappointment.

Wait, why was my first instinct to look for Meg not Amber? Amber was the girl of my dreams.

But now I felt like I was living a nightmare. I just want to wake up. The look on Amber's face said it all; Fear, Disgust, Horror and Disbelief. I could take no more. Pushing through the stunned crowd; I sprinted for the exit door.

Chapter 69
Fireman Kyle

Running through the crisp night air caused my aquatic features to dissolve, but it was all too late. My secret was out, and I was now branded a freak.

My manic, frantic running was taking me farther and farther away from the school. Looking from side to side, I didn't see any familiar buildings. I came to an abrupt stop. Not due to being out of breath, but because I was lost.

It's funny where one ends up when they don't know where they are going. I ran and ran and didn't look back. I didn't consciously know where I was headed; I just couldn't stay at school and continue to be ridiculed.

My heart literally ached. I believe this was a combination of having it broken by Amber's look of disgust, and my lack of cardio training.

I found myself in front of an unfamiliar house. Why had my feet led me here?

I stared at the house trying to collect my thoughts. Without warning, one of the small windows of the house blew out. Pieces of glass and curtain flew onto the lawn. Smoke billowed out of the broken window.

I should have jumped, or at least reacted in a manner that manifested shock, but I just continued to stare at the house. The front screen door flew open and someone appeared. The person had their back to me, and they were dragging something.

"Help!" the person screamed. "Help us!"

I snapped out of my fog and raced into action. Instantly, I was beside the person who had come out of the house.

"Let me help you."

"Kyle?" a familiar voice said.

Meg was bent over her mom, tears streamed down Meg's face. Her mom moved her arm, ever so slightly.

I didn't know where my strength came from, but I carefully picked up Meg's mom and took her to the farthest edge of the lawn from the house.

Meg knelt down beside her mom, who I had gently placed on the lawn. I had never heard Meg cry so hard. I looked up when I heard siren noises growing louder. Meg kept her face down, touching her mom's forehead with hers.

A neighbor from across the street ran over to us.

"Meg! Is she okay?"

Meg just continued to sob. The neighbor yelled to some other people who had gathered on the street. "Call an ambulance!"

The neighbor pointed at Meg's house and gasped. This time Meg looked up. Flames flickered outside the broken window. Meg put her hands over her face and collapsed onto her mom's shoulder. Her mom was breathing, but it didn't sound quite right.

"Don't cry, sweetie." Meg's mom's voice was barely a whisper. "You're safe."

It was at that moment I decided to embrace my powers. I am what I am for a reason. It was time to be me.

Without hesitation I stretched forth my hands. Water bubbled over the tops of the sprinklers that lined the sides of the lawn. A few seconds passed, and then suddenly streams of water shot out of sprinkler.

I focused on driving the water higher and higher, until it enveloped Meg's entire house. The neighbor beside me took a step back.

The flames coming out of the house grew larger. The sprinkler water wasn't enough. I focused and forced more water from the sprinklers.

The deluge only lasted a moment. The sprinklers sputtered and the streaming water fell to the ground. The sprinklers retracted into the ground and I was left without a water supply.

The deluge had mitigated the flames, but now that the house was not receiving any water, the flames were coming back with fury. I stepped back and shook my head in despair.

A tap on my shoulder started me. I slowly turned my head. It was the neighbor who was initially beside me when I set off the sprinklers. He simply pointed to red fire hydrant that was across the street.

My eyes widened. I gave the neighbor a sincere smile. He nodded and walked backwards to the crowd now gathered on the street.

I faced the crowd and was greeted with smiles and nods. This gave me courage.

Closing my eyes, I imaged the water gushing from the fire hydrant and drenching the house. My visualization was interrupted by oohs and awes from the crowd.

When I opened my eyes, the fire hydrant rocked back and forth. I intensified my concentration and the hydrant rocked even faster. Suddenly, BOOM! Like a rocket ship the hydrant shot into the air. Some neighbors screamed, others ran for cover, but some even cheered.

Focusing my power directly on the fountain of water shooting, I willed the water toward Meg's house. Like a snake the water entered through the broken window.

Since I couldn't see the inside the house, I made sure to direct streams of water in multiple directions.

Moments later the fire was out. The open hole where the fire hydrant was still had water coming out, but it was now bubbling over, and running down the street.

Exhausted, my arms flopped to my sides and I dropped to my knees by Meg. Meg looked at me, and shook her head.

"Kyle?"

I gave Meg a confident, reassuring smile. I wanted her to know it was all worth the risk.

I could hear murmuring behind me. I closed my eyes before turning to face the fate the crowd had in store for me. I was prepared to receive the same fate as Frankenstein's monster.

Chapter 70
Applause of Acceptance

With eyes closed, I heard light clapping. The clapping intensified to a feverish pitch. I opened my eyes to an enthusiastic crowd of neighbors, students from the dance, Principal Stern, Mary & Roger and of course Ian. They were all standing in the middle of the road, giving me thunderous applause.

What was going on? No torches and pitchforks? Obviously they had witness my display of supernatural power. They should be running me out of town, or they should be running for the hills.

Before my questions could be answered, the real firefighters arrived. The crowd ceased their applause, stepping back onto the sidewalk.

A fire truck and ambulance roared down the street. They pulled in front of Meg's house, cutting off my view of the once appreciative crowd.

After the professionals arrived on the scene, Meg's mom was carefully placed into the back of an ambulance. Meg never left her side. My heart ached as I watched the ambulance drive away.

A hand touched my shoulder, I flinched. Ian stood beside me; his eyes were filled with tears.

We looked at each in silence. Finally Ian gulped; put both his hands on my shoulders and looked deep into my eyes.

"You really are my hero bro."

Ian's genuine compliment caught me off guard. I stood speechless, just smiling at him.

"I agree son," came Roger's unmistakable voice.

"Me too," Mary affirmed.

All three embraced me.

Slowly High School students and strangers came up and thanked me for my heroics. All this attention was overwhelming. I began to blush and wanted to hide.

"We need to leave!" Grabbing my arm, Roger pulled me out from the crowd.

From the other side of the crowd a man with a pad of paper in one hand and a pen in the other. It seemed that he was attempting to push his way through the crowd, his eyes fixed on me. I smiled and waved. The man looked puzzled.

"Come on Kyle." This time his voice had more of a sense of urgency.

Before I knew it I was in Mary's Buick. "Who was that Roger?" I inquired.

"Trouble," Roger replied sternly. The drive home was quietly awkward. Mary and Roger kept giving each other worried glances. I should probably be worried but I was just happy Meg was safe.

Chapter 71
Okay, Now What?

Sun beams shined through the veiled curtains of my bedroom. I stared up at my cloud covered ceiling, pondering last night's conversation with Roger and Mary.

Roger said the man running toward us, with the notepad, was a slimy reporter for a local tabloid. Mary said the gentleman's name was Harold, and he wrote for the Red Rock Gazette.

My inquiry regarding the seemingly accepting crowd and their round of applause was met with Roger's comment of, "Folks around these parts have seen their share of the bizarre and strange."

Mary added she felt it was destiny, me coming to this very town, and finding them. Roger threw in a pun about me definitely surfacing in the right place.

They both reassured me that their friends and neighbors embraced the unique and mysterious.

Unique and mysterious? To me this was their polite way of saying weird.

I didn't want to get out of bed, but I could hear Mary and Roger talking outside my door. It was time to face the music. What was going to happen to me? Thrown back into the sea? Sent to the circus? Sold to a government lab? Phew, I'd been watching too much of the Syfy channel.

"Good morning," I cheerfully sang out, opening my bedroom door, but the hall was empty.

Where were Mary and Roger? I could still hear their voices.

"Hello?" I said walking down the hall to the kitchen. No one was visible; not in the kitchen, not in the living room, not anywhere. But their voices were still loud and clear.

"Where are you?" I hollered, feeling a little desperate.

I popped my ears with my fingers, and shook my head from side to side. I'd observed people using this technique to get excess water out of their ears. I thought it might help with my audio reception.

Searching through the house, I caught a glimpse of Mary and Roger standing outside, staring at the ocean. Perhaps they really were contemplating sending me back to the sea. Nevertheless, I needed to visit with them.

"Excuse me," I interrupted. "Is everything okay?"

Only Roger turned around. I could tell he had been crying. Mary must still be in the act of weeping, because she did not face me.

"Mamma?" I quietly said.

Roger put his arm around my shoulders, and directed me back up the path toward the house. "Give her a few minutes."

"I did something wrong, didn't I?" I hung my head in shame.

"Let's go on inside now." Roger escorted me to the house. Mary was still at the other end of the path, facing the sea.

I lay slumped over the breakfast table, staring blankly at the far wall.

"What would you like for breakfast, young man?" Roger feigned cheerfulness.

"The truth!" I retorted.

Roger set his frying pan on the counter, and joined me at the breakfast table. He cleared his throat, ready to talk, but I abruptly cut him off. "I've put you and Mary in danger, haven't I?"

Roger's pause gave me my answer.

"I knew it!"

I guess you could say I had a little temper tantrum. Mary would have called it "victimitis." Roger would have called it "crybabyitis."

Of course, he would have used that remark in jest, but I think he realized that right now, I wasn't in the mood for sarcasm.

I repeatedly pounded my fists on the table, before folding my arms and slamming them down on the table. With a heavy sigh I let my head flop onto my folded arms. I shook my bowed head back and forth while making whiny, groaning noises.

Roger cleared his throat. "Kyle, I ..."

I listened intently for Roger to complete his sentence, but he didn't. Instead with a voice expressing even deeper concern he said, "Mary?"

I raised my head. Mary leaned against the doorway to the kitchen, shaking so badly she almost dropped the cordless phone she was holding. Her eyes were swollen and full of tears.

"It's Meg's mom."

Chapter 72
Special K Delivery

Before I knew it all three of us were in Ol'Blue, heading to the hospital. I had watched some medical dramas on TV, so I was familiar with what I thought might be a real-life hospital. I was going to ask Mary and Roger if what I was about to see was life imitating art or were the shows art imitating life, but it seemed that no one wanted to speak just now.

I looked at the road in front of us that stretched toward the town and wondered "where this hospital was at?" My curiosity got the better of me and I quietly and politely asked, "Sir, will it take much longer?"

Roger and Mary both kept their eyes on the road in front of us. I looked at Roger and nodded my head in anticipation of his answer. Roger did a little shuffle in his seat. "Ten or so minutes I suppose."

"Thank you, sir." I wanted to be sarcastic, but Mary was fond of saying that there was no place for sarcasm in the Starr family.

I took a deep breath and was about to speak, but then made a new decision and remained silent. Mary also took a deep breath and gave her head a small shake. She then put her hand on my knee. "Oh Kyle, please speak freely."

"Are you sure?"

"Yes," Roger and Mary responded in unison.

"Why do you think the people and students reacted the way they did?"

"You mean when you extinguished the fire?"
I looked at the floor, a little embarrassed and ashamed.

"Yeah."

"Hmmm," said Mary. "That is a good question Kyle. I think it has to do with your..."

"Heart!" Roger blurted out.

"My heart?" I wasn't following.

"Miles and miles of it," Roger continued.

I sat in silence, attempting to process what Roger was getting at.

"It's pure." Mary interjected. "I think everyone can feel that."

"Plus," added Roger, "these folks around here have seen, or at least heard about sea creatures and mermaids."

"Roger." Mary elbowed Roger in the ribs.

"Careful woman, I'm drivin' here."

Roger looked over at me and grinned. "Don't go being ashamed of what you are Kyle, or the gifts that you got."
Mary put her arm around me and whispered in my ear.

"You are oh so, so special, Kyle. Everything is going to be okay."

I believed her, at least about the "everything is going to be okay" part. I wasn't sure about the special aspect. I just felt like a weirdo.

Chapter 73
Hydro Power

When we finally arrived at the hospital, I found Meg holding her mom's hand.

"I am so, so sorry, Meg," I said as I stepped through the door. Immediately, Meg sprang from her chair and wrapped her arms around me. Burying her face in my shoulder; Meg began to cry. Mary and Roger enclosed us both with a loving hug.

We all stood in the doorway, embracing for what seemed like an hour. I didn't mind so much, being that close to Meg that is, but the circumstance was tragic.

Once we'd all gained a bit of composure, we moved to the foot of Meg's mom's hospital bed.

In hushed tones, Meg explained that she found her mom passed out on the kitchen floor and whatever her mom had been cooking on the stove had set fire to the kitchen. The doctor had told Meg that Meg's mom's head injury and loss of oxygen due to the smoke inhalation caused Meg's mom to go into a coma.

"People recover from comas all the time, right?" Meg kept reassuring herself and us.

"Of course, dear," Mary continued to respond.

About 5% to 10% of all coma patients were incapable of conscious behavior, and ended up vegetative, which most of the public thought of as prolonged coma. At least that was what I remembered reading.

"She will be fine, Meg." I wasn't about to share my statistics with her.

Meg smiled at me and brushed her fallen hair out of her face. A strange sensation filled my belly, kind of an ill but yet pleasant feeling.

I was still processing when Meg took my hand and gently guided me to the side of her mom's bed. "Please hold her hand, Kyle."

"What?" I had only met Mrs. Dawson on one other occasion and frankly I didn't think she had approved of me being her daughter's friend. Meg crinkled her face at me and released my hand. "I mean why?" I tried a softer approach.

"Kyle," Mary gently chided. I looked at Mary who had a look of "now Kyle" on her face. My eyes darted to Roger and he gently nodded. I knew what that meant. It meant, "Do the right thing, son".

I let out a little sigh and reached toward Mrs. Dawson's hand.

"Never mind!" Meg's annoyed voice caught me off guard. I didn't know someone could anger whisper so forcefully.

"Don't do me any favors." Meg continued to voice her displeasure toward me in hushed but harsh tones.

"I..."

Meg she turned her back on me and wept.

Mary immediately came over to Meg and embraced her with another loving hug. I gulped and looked at Roger. He motioned toward Mrs. Dawson using his head.

I looked over at Mrs. Dawson's lifeless form, and cringed. I looked back at Roger who gave me a definitive nod. I paused, closed my eyes and mentally gathered my courage.

Thoughts of any form of coma treatment raced through my mind. Multiple articles appeared and then faded from my mental view. Then one article I recalled seeing at some point in time froze as if I'd hit a pause button in my brain.

The research was about aquatic therapy and hydrostatic pressure having a calming effect on the body and brain. The study conducted was focused on relieving the cycle of pain, depression and stress from traumatic brain injury, but I had a confident feeling that if I manipulated the water in Mrs. Dawson's body, I could reduce the time it would take her to recover from her coma.

I opened my eyes and found Meg, Mary, and Roger staring at me, somewhat amazed. I realized I had been holding tight to Mrs. Dawson's hand. Even though her eyes were closed still, she didn't look as lifeless anymore. It almost looked like she had a slight smile on her face.

"What did you say to her?" Meg asked, taking a step toward me.

"Huh?" I released Mrs. Dawson's hand and stepped away from her bed.

"What language was that?"

"Language?" I had no idea what Meg was referencing.

"Kyle, dear," Mary interjected. "We best let Meg have some alone time with her mom."

"Yeah, okay." I brushed past Meg and joined Mary and Roger who had now made their way to the door.

Meg pulled a chair next to her mom's bed and clasped her mom's hand in both her hands. Meg studied her mom's face for a moment and then looked over at me. "Thank you."

"Sure thin," I said sheepishly.

Roger put his arm around my shoulder and began to escort me out of the room.

"Kyle," Meg called out. I cringed, hoping there would be no more compliments or questions. "You can tell Ian."

"What?" I was a bit confused.

"About my mom being here. He doesn't know yet."

"Will do," I nodded. "Take care." I turned away, letting the door shut behind us.

On the drive home, I watched the rain run down Ol' Blue's window. A brilliant rainbow lit up the sky. I had a newfound respect for water. In its rain form it could cause growth and it could also be the cause of much devastation.

I really didn't know what happened with Mrs. Dawson, but I felt drained and I knew I had exerted some type of healing power on her brain.

Mary and Roger didn't ask me about what I'd said or what I'd done; they both just sat in silence with pleased expressions on their faces.

Chapter 74
The Power of Belief

Superhero!" exclaimed Ian.

Ian had been waiting on the front steps of the lighthouse when we arrived home. Now inside in front of a warm fireplace, and sipping Roger's famous hot cocoa, Ian continued his pontification.

"You are like Aquaman and the Submariner combined!" He paused for a moment to think. He snapped his fingers. "With a dash of Percy Jackson thrown into the mix."

"Wow, thanks," I said. "I know there are some females who are pretty sweet on the Jackson fellow."

Roger nudged Ian. "Isn't that Aquaman kind of a wimp? Superfriends and all."

"Maybe back in the day, Mr. Starr, but in the New 52 he kicks some serious-"

"Ian!" Mary warned.

"Ooops, sorry Mrs. S." Ian began vigorously sipping his hot cocoa.

I put my mug down on the hearth of the fireplace. "We shouldn't get our hopes up Ian."

Ian looked up.

"Why would you say that?" Ian's question oozed with disappointment.

I gulp, having been caught off guard. "I'm just trying to be realist-"

"No!" Ian cut me off with an abrupt and defiant rebuke.

Stunned, I looked at Mary and Roger for support. Roger gave me one of his shoulder shrugs, which usually meant it was up to me.

Mary rested her head on Roger's shoulder and smiled lovingly at me. I definitely knew that Mary's smile meant, "give Ian something to hope for."

During the time I had spent with the Starrs, I'd learned to read the nonverbal cues.

"Hydro Power!" I exclaimed.

Ian's eyes widened and he slowly brought his mug away from his mouth-"What?"

I leaned forward and gave Ian a serious and concentrated look.

"Empty your mind."

Ian's mug hit the table.

I continued, "Be formless. Shapeless. Like water."

Now mesmerized, Ian leaned forward.

"Ian," I said with a little more force. "You put water into a cup and it becomes the cup." I made a shape of a cup with my hands. "You put water into a bottle and it becomes the bottle." Now with both hands I formed an imaginary bottle in the air. "Water can flow or it can crash." I sat back in my chair. "Be water, my friend."

Ian opened his mouth so wide that his half-chewed marshmallow fell out and plopped back into his hot chocolate.

"That was incredible."

"Thanks," I said modestly.

Ian shook his head. "How? Where did you…"

Roger walked by and patted me on the shoulder. "Nice work."

I pointed up at Roger with my thumb. "He's a big fan." Ian looked at Roger and nodded.

"Whaaaa!" Roger let out his version of Mr. Lee's iconic yell, as he left the room.

"Easy, Bruce," Mary called after him.

Ian spun around and looked at Mary in shock, obviously surprised that Mary knew the reference also. Mary winked at Ian as she followed Roger into the next room.

Ian put down his mug of hot chocolate and raised his hands high above his head. "Your folks are awesome!"

I looked in the direction that Mary and Roger had gone and smiled. "Yeah, they are."

"Wow!" Ian continued, clasping his hands behind his head. "This is awesome!" Ian leaned forward about to speak, then paused and looked around the room before coming back to me. Ian leaned in even closer and whispered, "Do you really think your water manipulation mojo is going to cure Mrs. Dawson?"

Keep positive, Kyle. Keep positive Kyle. I leaned closer to Ian and stared him straight in the eyes, cleared my throat, and in my deepest baritone voice said, "I find your lack of faith disturbing."

Ian's eyes looked like they were going to pop out of their sockets. Yes, Ian was not only a connoisseur of superheroes and all things comics, but Ian was an avid fan of StarWars also.

Before Ian could speak, Roger triumphantly entered the kitchen.

"Hey!" Roger proudly said, holding up today's newspaper. "Told ya all I have connections." Roger gently placed the newspaper in front of Ian and me, as if it was a fragile china dish.

"Whoa," said Ian. Then paused and frowned. "Ahhh, dang it."

Before Mary could utter her usual "Mr. Kennedy, please clean up your language," Ian quickly spun his head in her direction.

"Sorry Mrs. S. Please forgive me."

Mary's mouth was slightly open as if she was about to speak. She closed her mouth, smiled at Ian, and gave him a tinkling wink of her eyes. Ian grinned widely.

The newspaper article featured an artist rendition of what was supposed to be me in an adult size fish costume. The caption above the picture said, "Fish Boy a Hoax." I scrunched up my face and in a disappointed tone said, "This is good right?"

"See!" Ian shouted, "Kyle thinks it's lame too, I can tell."

"Hmm," Roger said picking up the paper. Mary peered over his shoulder.

"Well, it isn't the most flattering picture ever." Mary remarked.

Roger tossed the paper back on the table. "You all are missing the point." Roger seemed a little exasperated. The room went quiet.

"I get it," I gleefully announced. "This means I can go to school and see Amber!"

"I knew you'd catch on," Roger said, patting my shoulder.

"You'll need to call us right away if there is any trouble," Mary added.

I smiled with glee.

"What!?" Ian stood up from the table. "Has everyone lost their minds?" Ian didn't wait for a response. "The enemy is still out there." Now Ian was pacing around the kitchen. "We can just rush back into the battlefield." Ian paused and looked at each one of us. "You feel me?"

Mary's eyes widened and Roger cleared his throat. Roger placed his hand on Ian's shoulder, forcing Ian to stop frantically moving and inquired, "So, what's the plan, General?"

Ian nodded and gave a sly grin. "We need to be covert. We need to be stealthy...We need disguises!"

Chapter 75
Best Incognito Ever

Ol' Blue sat parked outside the local indoor pool facility. Roger, Ian, and I sat in the truck looking at the entrance to the pool.

"Well, you doin' this or not?" Ian impatiently asked.

I gulped and look down at my outfit. Roger looked over and did his best to cover up his snicker. I was adorned in Mary's red rubber boots, Roger's were too big for me, and a long lime green raincoat. We couldn't find a hat to match, so I used one of Roger's fishing hats. We'd stopped by Ian's on the way to the pool so he could get his long red wig that looked more like an orange hippie wig, and a pair of his mom's "Hollywood" sunglasses.

"Put the shades on and go," Ian demanded. "We ain't got all night."

"It's dark out," I answered. "Why do I need the sunglasses?"

Ian promptly snatched the sunglasses out of my hands and poked both lenses out.

"Whoa," I said in horror.

"Don't worry," Ian said. "Mom's got like fifty of these things."

Ian handed the glasses back to me and motioned for me to put them on.

I reluctantly slipped them on and looked at Roger.

"Better?"

Roger's eyes widened. "Who are you? How'd you get in my truck?"

"Told ya!" Ian exclaimed. "Now go get 'em."

I rolled my eyes. Roger chuckled and patted me on the shoulder. "Good luck, son."

I opened the truck door and mumbled under my breath, "Wish I had my Elvis outfit."

"What?" Ian asked.

"Nothing."

I stepped out and closed the truck door. Slowly, I walked in front of the truck and I was sure that the headlights illuminated my outfit for everyone to see. I took a deep breath and headed toward the indoor pool entrance.

"No fear, no fear," I heard coming from behind me. I looked over my shoulder to see Ian leaning over Roger and calling out the window. Roger calmly pushed Ian back in his seat and rolled up the window.

I got quite a few odd looks and giggles from young kids as I walked through the front doors of the indoor pool building. After a few moments of surveying the room, I saw her.

Amber was at the end of the pool, keeping guard over several little children who were splashing through the water. The reflection from the pool illuminated Amber's face and hair giving her that, "oh so familiar" angelic look. Wow, this was going to be tough.

Amber looked up and our eyes met. Wait, did she recognize me?

Another life guard took her place at the end of the pool and Amber walked toward me. How could she have known it was me? I looked around, wondering if she was meeting someone else, but when I looked back at her, she gave me an odd smile and kept walking toward me.

Phew, the moment of truth; seemed like I'd been having quite a few of those lately. I supposed I should have met her halfway, but my feet didn't want to move. The closer she came to me, the more I began to think this was not such a stellar idea.

"Kyle?" Amber's voice was as sweet as usual, but I could tell there was some hesitation.

"Hello, Amber." My voice shook. "Please don't be afraid."

"I'm not," she said reassuringly. "What's with the costume?"

"Ian's idea," I said. "Thought it'd be safer this way."

Amber led me to a quieter corner of the pool area.

"How did you know?" I said as we walked.

"Your eyes are a dead give-away."

"Oh," I said. My face was probably as red as the fake hair I was wearing.

"You might want to change if you're going in." Amber nodded toward the pool.

I laughed nervously. "Oh no, I actually came to speak with you."

Amber tilted her head and put her hands on her hips.

"About the story in the paper?"

"What?" Now I was confused.

"I don't get the joke," Amber continued. "Was Brad in on it?"

"Sort of, I mean, I want to talk about me and what happened." I hoped I wasn't sounding pretentious.

Amber softly touched my wrist. I visibly shivered. "It's okay. I know who you are, Kyle, and I like it."

If I am dreaming, please nobody pinch me.

Chapter 76
Paparazzi Attack

You are the kinda guy who stands up for his friends. You're not afraid of what other people think."

Amber's words were a welcome reprieve. I really wasn't sure what she was going to say. My mind was still numbed by her touch, but I came to come clean. I steadied my courage. She needed to know who I really was, not that I even really knew.

I took a deep breath and squeezed her hand. The corner of her mouth lifted. "I am very different, Amber."

"Okay?" Amber squeezed my hand back which increased my level of nervousness exponentially.

"What I mean is, what happened at the dance," I swallowed hard. "It was-"

"A really weird prank?" Amber said hopefully.

"No, it wasn't."

Amber took a step away from me and looked justifiably perplexed. I needed to just come out and say it; I was some sort of "amphibian boy".

"What is going on, Kyle?" I could tell Amber's patience was getting thin. She unexpectedly grabbed both my hands. "Kyle, tell me!'"

I felt numb, like I was floating on top of the sea. My instincts told me I could trust her. "Amber, I am a ..."

BEEP! The blast from Ol'Blue's horn startled both of us. In unison, we looked toward the front doors. Swirling bright lights bounced on the translucent windows of the front doors. Strange jabbering noises grew louder as the lights got closer.

BEEP! Ol'Blue's horn sounded again. Was Roger trying to warn us? Was this going to be one of those alien abductions Ian had told me about? The doors burst open. "That's him!" a familiar, yet unwelcome voice shouted.

"Brad?" Amber said with disdain.

Brad led a procession of news reporters and cameras straight toward me. Flashes of lights blinded me.

"Is it true?" "Who are you?" "Where did you come from?" "Can you show us?" A barge of questions were thrown at me from various reporters.

The reporters and cameramen crowded around us, pushing Amber and I closer together. If the circumstances had been different, I would have quite enjoyed the proximity Amber and I were in, but this was a media circus.

Panic bubbled to the surface. Amber gave Brad a stern look of disapproval. He just sneered at us in return.

Emancipation came when Roger's two strong hands gripped my shoulders. "Let's get you two outta here."

Roger led us through the labyrinth of reporters and to the truck. "Let the boy alone, it's just a skin condition".

Ian leaned out the window, frantically waving for us to keep coming, just like someone guiding an airplane down the runway. Safe in our vessel, we sped away from the frenzied crowd of new people who had now turned their attention on Brad.

"Phew. Now you know how Tony Stark must have felt."

I couldn't help but chuckle at Ian's comic book references.

"So, you're a Marvel fan?" Amber said.

All of us, including Roger, looked at Amber with stunned expressions.

"Whoa" was all Ian came out with.

"I'll admit; it's a pretty cool universe. DC however, they have the big three," Amber continued. Ian's jaw dropped.

"Oh, I know this one!" I exclaimed. "Batman, Superman, and huh, the Lasso Lady."   Amber gave me a gentle pat on the knee, which of course I wouldn't complain about.

"Wonder Woman." Amber was kind with her correction. I smiled. "*Yes, yes you are.*"

At the lighthouse, Amber used the "landline" since her cellphone was left at the indoor pool. She wanted to let her parents know she was okay. Roger, Mary, Ian, and I sat around the kitchen table.

"She doesn't know?" Mary was concerned.

"I don't think so. I mean, I tried to tell her and then, all bedlam broke loose."

Ian tipped back on his chair. "Kyle, sometimes you kill me."

"All six feet on the floor please, Ian." Mary's rebuke was gentle.

"Yes, Mrs. S." Ian carefully sat forward and Mary gave him a nod of approval.

"Well, you best tell that gal something," said Roger. "She's a keeper."

"Who's a keeper?" Amber said walking into the kitchen.

Everyone was immediately silent.

"Could I talk to you?" I stood up from the table and faced Amber.

"Of course."

"Let's go in the family room." I led Amber by the hand into the family room. She didn't seem to mind because she kept a hold of my hand as we stood in front of the roaring fire.

"Amber."

"Yes?"

"I need to show you, well, what I think I am always supposed to look like. Please give me a moment to prepare a solution of water and salt. If you would be kind enough to wait here, then I'll..."

"Stop Kyle, you don't need to show me anything."

"I don't?"

"No. I learned long ago that it's what's on the inside that matters."

"Oh."

"And you, Kyle Starr, are great."

Amber embraced me. For a moment I stood frozen, then slowly my arms wrapped around her. This was one of the most tender hugs I'd ever experienced.

"Huh, guys, I think you better see this." Ian's voice had a serious tone, one I'd heard only once before. Ian ushered Amber and I to a window that overlooked the beach. Mary and Roger were already looking out the window in awe.

When the lighthouse beam struck the beach, three figures were revealed. Their silver hair sparkled. They were carrying some sort of spears and large forks. The pace of their walk said that they meant business. I stepped back from the window and looked at my family and friends.

"They are here for me."

Chapter 77
Kingdom Calling

It was just like a scene from the old western TV shows that Roger watched. On one side stood Roger, Mary, Ian, Amber and I, and about fifteen feet away from us stood our ocean dwelling visitors; two muscular stern looking males and a beautiful, also stern looking, female. Their silver, shiny hair was turning brown, black and blonde, respectively.

Even though I felt anxious, I knew these beings were not here to cause me or my family and friends harm. I steeled my courage and glanced at Amber. "I better greet them."

Amber squeezed my hand. "Be careful."

That was all I needed. I boldly stepped toward the three strangers. With each step that took me closer to my target, my thoughts began to betray my emotions.

"What am I doing?" I mumbled.

Three fierce appearing adults from another world were standing in front of me, all holding long, spear-like weapons of some kind. After an involuntary swallow, I looked back at my group and forced what I hoped came across as a reassuring smile.

Standing within five feet of the warriors caused my knees to tremble. Their piercing blue eyes were similar to mine. Any remains of silver hair were now completely gone and their scales had vanished.

"Greetings," I said. "Welcome to the town of Red Rock."

The trio simultaneously stepped forward. *Relax, Kyle, they mean you no harm.* I forced the thought into my mind. They knelt down on one knee. I stood frozen. This wasn't a collapse from exhaustion; this was some sort of sign of respect. Majestically, they bowed their heads and raised their weapons high, and in unison said what sounded like the word "righ."

The synapses of my brain fired, attempting to translate their language. Then as if someone had turned up a dial in my mind, I understood what "righ" meant: *A member of a royal family, who is a supreme ruler of a nation.*

Wait... what... me? I jolted as an arm hugged me across my back.

"Looks like you got yourself a fan club," Roger whispered through clenched teeth. "Best invite them in. Passersby may get too curious for our good."

We congregated in Mary's kitchen. This was too weird. Roger was right; this would have been a million-dollar photo for one of those tabloid magazines.

Our three guests sat across the table from me. Brown hair poked the marshmallows in his hot chocolate. He smiled as they bobbed up and down.

Blondie carefully sipped on her cocoa. I could tell by the look in her eyes that she wanted to reveal a grin of delight, but she managed to keep her rigid composure.

Black hair, the obvious leader, had his hands cupped around his hot chocolate mug. He looked directly in my eyes, no blinking, and no flinching. It felt like something was pounding on the door to my mind, either to take something out or bring something in. His gaze became more intense and without warning an acute pain slashed through my skull.

"Ahhh!" I cupped my hands on each of my temples, rocking from side to side. Amber, who was standing behind me, put her hands on my shoulders. "Kyle, have him stop. This is hurting you."

Black hair sat back in his chair and sighed. Recovering from his mind blast, I shook my head. "I am sorry." Black hair looked at his companions, then back at me. In rapid fire succession they all began speaking at me.

"Whoa, whoa," I said. "Too fast."

They abruptly stopped and frowned at me in disappointment.

"I know I should understand you, but I can't. Once again, I apologize."

"Fresh baked cookies," Mary announced as she placed a plate of delicious oatmeal chocolate chip cookies in the center of the table. Mary smiled at the three and motioned for them to partake.

Once Black hair retrieved a cookie, took a bite, and gave a genuine nod of approval, the other two dove right in.

"Figured you all needed a break." Mary winked at me.

She was handling this strange occurrence with such poise. I guess having me as a son helped her prepare for the bizarre side of life. Suddenly, I realized that Roger and Ian were not in the room. I looked around the kitchen and into the adjacent family room. They were nowhere in sight. Before I could inquire as to their whereabouts, Amber knelt down by my side.

"Hey." Her voice was soft and reassuring. "You'll figure this out."

"Thanks. This must be very unorthodox for you."

"You mean strange?" Amber smiled. "To tell you the truth, I am still trying to process it."

"I'm sorry."

She took my hand and stood back up. "Quit apologizing. Everything will work out." My heart began to race. This was the longest period of time that our hands had ever remained intertwined. "Hmm," she said.

"What is it?"

Amber whispered in my ear, her lips barely touching. This was not helping me concentrate, but I enjoyed every moment. "Why don't you just speak with the girl?"

"You think so?" Amber moved back behind my chair, giving me a wink on the way. I cleared my throat.

"Excuse me." There was no response. They were too involved in cookie consumption.

This time I coughed loudly, then boldly announced. "I need your attention please!" With chocolate covered lips and teeth, my guests stared at me in surprise. I simply smiled. "I'd like to address you," I said pointing at Blondie. She looked at Black hair.

"Please don't tell me they are from a male dominant society," Amber said under her breath. I couldn't help but smile.

I sat up straight and took fresh courage. "It is apparent that all of you hold me in some type of high regard. I am flattered, I guess, but I need to know two things. Who am I, and why are you here?"

I knew Blondie understood what I wanted, even if she couldn't translate my English into her native tongue.

"Wait a minute," I said. "I can speak English. Why can't you? Or can you?" With wide eyes she looked to her dark-haired leader.

"Hey! You don't need permission. Just tell me." My tone was sharp and firm.

Blondie smiled and began to chatter. I put my hands forward and indicated for her to slow down. My mind was frantically attempting to decipher her words. *Come on. I got the word "righ", let me understand her.* This was a language that I once must have spoken fluently. Why not now?

"Okay, okay." I said. "Let's take a break. I am not getting anything."

Amber gently rubbed my arm. "It'll happen, Kyle." Her smile was soft and warm. "Maybe if we knew what language this was."

"It's a form of ancient Scottish Gaelic," a familiar voice from behind us spoke up.

"Meg!" I spun around, jumped off my seat, and I gave Meg a huge hug. Ian and Roger came around the corner and flashed us smiles.

"Figured we better get super brain in here, and figure this thing out." Ian's pride in Meg could not be masked. Meg curtsied and laughed. All three visitors stared at Meg with curiosity. Meg pulled a chair out and sat close to Blondie.

"May I?" Meg's inquiry was directed at me.

I nodded graciously. "Do your thing."

Chapter 78
Meg the Magnificent

Meg placed a pad of paper and pen in front of the female. Blondie snatched up the pen and began to scribble. She paused for a moment and glanced at Black Hair out of the corner of her eye, then gave a slight smile and continued. Within moments, the pad was full of ancient looking symbols.

"Hmm," Meg said. "She is a clever one."

"Do you know what it says?" I inquired.

"She has hidden English letters within the symbols," Meg answered.

"Sly fox." Ian giggled.

Blondie gave Ian a genuine smile. Ian gulped, and his face turned a little red.

"It seems that they can speak English," Meg continued. "They are just forbidden."

"Chan eil!" Black Hair said, pounding the table. Brown Hair dropped his cookie. All of us dared not move.

"Now, now, we don't hit the table," Mary put one hand on Black Hair's closed fist. He winced. "This must be frustrating for you, but you are safe here."

Wow, was this magnificent woman afraid of anything? Black Hair smiled respectfully at Mary, and his fist relaxed. Obviously, he had a loving mother too.

"That was awkward," Ian's understated comment made us all laugh nervously.

"Shall we get back to business?"

Meg seemed undaunted, but her tapping foot told me otherwise. Regardless, Meg was amazing. It took quite a lot of effort, but she was somehow able to communicate with our new friends

"Lost Prince?" I felt embarrassed.

"You're like Simba." Ian snickered.

"I knew you were special," Amber smiled and the usual warm feeling stirred inside my chest.

"Are you positive that's what they-"

"Scottish Gaelic is made up of eighteen letters, Meg said. "Traditionally the letters of the alphabet were named after trees."

I was stunned and looked at Ian.

He shook his head. "It's her thing."

"Sorry, Meg, I didn't mean to doubt you."

"No worries. I did my due diligence and discovered that the Atlanteans have a lineage that dates back to the ancient Highland Scots."

Meg cleared her throat. The corner of her mouth rose slightly. I think she was very pleased with herself. She should have been, I was impressed and Ian was beaming with pride.

"Sorry for the interjection, Meg dear, but what else did they say about Kyle?" Mary gentle interrupted.

Meg adjusted her glasses and shifted in her chair. "Basically, they'll be back to collect him in a fortnight."

"What?" Mary was stunned.

"Fortnight!" yelled Roger. "That's two weeks."

If the situation hadn't just become so volatile I think everyone would have taken notice of how impressive it was the Roger knew a Scottish term, but everyone started talking at once and the visitors began to look agitated.

"What do they mean collect him?" Amber insisted.

"Kyle isn't going anywhere!" Ian shouted.

"Hey!" Meg was getting irritated now. "Don't shoot the messenger."

Chapter 79
Broken Hearts

The three guests spewed forth words at Ian and Amber. Of course, none of us knew what they were saying. Well, maybe Meg caught a few things here and there. She did gasp and cover her mouth a couple of times. I looked to Mary for guidance. Her tear-filled eyes told me this wasn't the time to ask her anything. I stood up to hug Mary and unexpectedly Roger's booming voice shook the room. "That's enough!"

I was so shocked that I immediately sat down. Roger wasn't one for confrontations, let alone raising his voice. Even the Atlanteans sat in reverent silence. All eyes were on Roger. He cleared his throat and put his shoulders back. After what seemed like an eternal pause, I didn't know whether it was for dramatic effect out of nervousness, Roger addressed his audience.

"We are sailing in uncharted waters here, friends." Roger looked at the Atlanteans and nodded. They returned his gesture. "Kyle is special beyond our comprehension. He is of pure heart and authentic character."

I was slightly embarrassed. Mary moved to Roger's side and put her arm around his waist. Amber looked at me and smiled. I smiled back and my peripheral vision caught the Atlanteans observing our exchange. Roger continued, this time a little choked up. "We've been blessed to have Kyle enter our lives and we've cherished every moment. Now, if he needs to go back and be with his people, there must be a very good reason. He surely is as important to them as he is to us."

With that, Roger turned and left the room. I attempted to follow him, but Mary advised me to let him be for a moment.

After some awkward attempts at good-bye handshakes and partial hugs between us and our guests, Mary suggested Meg and I walk them to the shore. Amber and Ian didn't seem on board with that recommendation, but acquiesced to Mary's request. Meg wanted to stay and talk with them, and since she could, somewhat, speak Atlantean; it seemed like an acceptable scenario.

Chapter 80
Farewell Is Not Goodbye

Three days had passed since my "kinfolk," the name Ian used to refer to our Atlantean visitors, had come and gone. Awkward and strange are good words to describe these last few days. Mary and Roger gave me permission to "skip" school if I so desired. However, I felt it best that I still attend and try to maintain some type of normal behavior. Normal, I supposed, was a relative term for a boy from Atlantis.

School turned out to be quite a melancholy event. Amber, Meg, and Ian seemed to be constantly on the verge of tears.

"Let's enjoy these moments together," I encouraged.

Ian kept his head bowed low and poked his green cafeteria Jell-O with a fork.

"Friends," I said hoping for more than just a blank stare. "We'll always be friends."

Ian shoved his Jell-O away. "Yeah right!"

I reached out a hand of brotherhood, but Ian recoiled and quickly stood up.

"Just go back to the sea where you belong."

Ian stormed out of the cafeteria and I was left wide eyed, looking for some reaction from the students around me. There was a brief pause and a momentary silence in their conversation, but soon they were all back to their idle chatter. I released a deep breath and wiped my brow. I knew Ian didn't mean what he'd said. He was just hurting inside as I was.

At the end of school, I sat on the bleachers looking out at the empty Red Rock Roosters football field. My thoughts were of my family, friends and my impending journey back to Atlantis. I wished I didn't have to go, but my instincts were telling me it was my duty.

How could I be a Prince of Atlantis if I couldn't even remember who I really was? Help a civilization I couldn't even remember? Why? I had a lovely family and friends that needed me here.

"Hey, Kyle."

The sound of Amber's voice was so sweet. "How are you holding up?"

She was the first person to ask me how I was coping with all of this.

I couldn't answer her question directly for fear of an emotional breakdown. "You know, I never got to see a game."

Amber laughed. "I've certainly cheered at my fair share of them."

"Big fan then?"

"Part of my job." Sensing my confusion, Amber continued, "Yep, I was cheer captain once."

"Wow. That must have been quite the honor."

Amber smiled. "I guess. All our efforts didn't help our losing team though. Worst record in the state."

"I bet you were great, though."

Amber took my hand and gave it a gentle squeeze. I swallowed hard. "Is that when you and Brad were, um, dating?"

Amber looked deep into my eyes. "Oh Kyle, you are one of a kind."

Amber took my face in her hands and gave me a gentle kiss, a kiss that seemed to last forever. I certainly wished it could have.

Chapter 81
Brother in Arms

Dinner with Mary and Roger was much more silent than usual. Usually, someone had a funny story or anecdote to share. I was wishing I'd invited Amber over, or Meg, or even angry Ian.

"Can we please talk about something?" I pleaded, "The silence is deafening."

"Ha." Roger reacted. That was progress. "You've been reading too many books."

"Can one really read too much, dear?" Mary asked.

"You're darn tootin'!"

Mary smiled at me, and then raised an eyebrow at Roger. "How so, dear?"

"Well, let's see," Roger continued. "If all this reading keeps a person's head in the clouds, they may forget to do the essentials of life."

Mary put her elbows on the table, interlocked her fingers and rested her chin on her hands. "Continue."

If I were Roger, I would have chosen my next words carefully. Of course, that was not Roger's style.

"If books interfere with a man getting his dinner time, well, then that's too much readin'."

A desperate pounding rattled the door. We sat motionless. The previous week's run-in with the unsolicited paparazzi had caused us all to be leery of opening doors to unannounced visitors.

"I'll get it." Roger stuck out his chest as he walked out of the kitchen. Mary reached over and squeezed my hand. There was a moment of pause then Roger yelled. "Come quick!"

Brown Hair lay slumped against the door frame. Lacerations and bruises marked him from head to toe. He reached up toward me. "My king, help me."

We carefully placed Brown Hair on the couch. Mary attended to his wounds. Roger paced back and forth, grinding his fist into his palm. I sat across from Brown Hair, contemplating my next question.

"What about..." I hesitated. "What about your friends? Are they injured too? Do we go and help them?"

Brown Hair's eyes were wet with tears. He shook his head and looked away from me. I couldn't sense whether that meant they were alive or not. A lump grew in my throat.

It didn't take a lot of prodding before Brown Hair related what had happen. I think he really wanted to try out his English, even though he was quite rusty, and it was apparent. After listening, restating, and validating Mary, Roger, and I were able to ascertain what led Brown Hair to return to our doorstep.

Mary, Roger, and I sat on the couch, while Brown Hair shared his tale with us. He was very enthusiastic and animated, quite a good storyteller. We were captivated, even though his narrative was a tragic one.

Brown Hair explained that he and his companions had been branded as "traitors" for coming to find me. The ruling monarch, upon discovering their treachery, sentenced them to death. If I didn't return now, Black Hair and Blondie would be killed as a public reminder that disloyalty to the government would not be tolerated.

"Will you return with me and emancipate our people?" Brown Hair's words were gentle but desperate.

I closed my eyes and nodded. Mary instantly broke into tears.

Roger hugged Mary, then abruptly stood up. "I've got some calls to make." Roger left the room and I held Mary tight in my arms. Brown Hair knelt in front of Mary and took her hands in his.

"I am Zenix Lar."

My eyes widened and Mary looked at Zenix through tear-filled eyes. It was like a scene from one of Edgar Rice Burroughs' books.

"It is forbidden for me to reveal our true names to those that dwell on land." Zenix smiled at Mary. "I should not even be speaking your native tongue, but I can feel that you truly love your son, my king, and you need to know."

Mary and I both looked at each other and then back and Zenix. "You son's name is Sandryan Lar." Zenix began to cry. He gripped my arm. "Kyle," he said with a slight grin. "I am your brother."

Jaws dropped. I fell back onto the couch. Mary stared at Zenix in shock, then flung her arms around him. "Bless you, Zenix, bless you."

"Done!" Roger announced as he came into the room.

"They've all been called."

Roger surveyed the room. Seeing his precious Mary so distraught pulled at his heartstrings. "We'll all get through this, my love." Roger choked back his tears.

Chapter 82
Return to the Sea

Assembled on the beach were all the people in my life that meant the most to me. Well, almost all of them.

"Well *Little King*, I guess this is goodbye." Meg held me close. According to Meg's Gaelic translation, which of course she assured us all is never wrong; my Atlantean name was made up of two parts. Sandy meant, *defender of man*, and Ryan meant, *little king*.

"Goodbye," I whispered in her ear, "… is not farewell."

Meg gave me one more very tight squeeze. Without warning, she kissed me on the cheek before stepping back.

"Meg," I said dumbfounded.

She punched my shoulder, briskly turned around, and walked back to Mary and Roger. They all embraced. Mary and Roger had been the first to hug me goodbye, multiple times. I think they had hugged themselves out.

Amber approached me next. Zenix patiently waited for me, waist deep in the ocean. His face shone with delight as he witnessed how much I was loved.

Amber's face was perfect, a combination of beauty and elegance. Her smile melted me. The setting sun illuminated her soft, golden strands. Her hair perfectly framed her face. I was so entranced that I barely noticed she was holding something behind her back.

"This is for you." Amber presented me with a comic encased in a plastic bag. "He left it on my doorstep."

The lump in my throat grew larger as I looked at Ian's handmade comic. I was on the cover, wearing some very stylish armor and holding a scepter. The title of the comic was, My Friend from Atlantis by Ian Kennedy. I choked on my tears.

Amber hugged me.

"Oh Kyle, I will miss you."

"I will miss you as well."

She held my hands and we touched foreheads. Nothing more could be said. It was all in our subtext. Zenix cleared his throat. "It is time, Sandryan."

Amber smiled at the sound of my Atlantean name. She gave me one last hug and returned to my group of loved ones.

Be strong Kyle, be strong. I stepped into the water and joined Zenix. Almost instantly, my body changed. I felt a surge of renewed power and strength. Tiny scales manifested themselves all over my body. I could feel the webbed skin form between my fingers and toes. My reflection in the water now showed a different boy than I was used to seeing in my bedroom mirror. My silver hair made me smile. This was strange, but somehow, I knew it was right.

"Ready?" Zenix said.

"Ready," I nodded.

Mary sprinted into the water and wrapped her arms around me. "I love you Kyle, I love you so much."

My heart broke. "Love you, Mom."

I wish I could have held Mary forever. When finally and regrettably disengaged from our embrace, we saw a figure standing above the beach on the cliff. It was Ian. He was draped in a red cape and had goggles covering his eyes.

"Ian!" I shouted, but I didn't think he could hear me over the crashing of the surf.

Ian stood at attention. He gave me a resolute salute. I saluted in return. Putting his hands to his side, Ian did an about-face and was gone. I would miss my dear friend and confidant.

Roger helped Mary out of the water. Mary, Roger, Meg, and Amber stood on the shore as Zenix and I disappeared into the water.

Once submerged, my loved ones on the beach looked distorted, like the figures from a dream.

I could hear Zenix's thoughts in my mind. "*Our journey to Hadal has begun, my brother.*"

I was leaving my home a boy and returning to my realm a king.

Chapter 83
Beyond Betrayal

Our journey was interminable; first through choppy waves, then through clear blue water, then dark blue water and finally into darkness. I thought the abyss wouldn't end.

Finally, bursting through the darkness were the bright lights of a magnificent, enormous, underwater city. My breath would have been taken away, if I didn't have to hold it in order to survive this ominous trip. This was the city that I had flashes of in my dreams.

Was I really coming home? I looked at my brother and smiled. Zenix's face was detached, yet from his strokes in the water his body looked strong and energetic. I, on the other hand, was exhausted.

What I wouldn't give right now to be in my rocket ship pajamas while I sat on Mary and Roger's comfy couch enjoying some hot cocoa.

Atlantis was encased in some sort of bubble. It was a force field that we were approaching. "*This may feel a little uncomfortable,*" Zenix projected into my mind.

"*Remember*?" I didn't remember, but my memory was about to receive a jolt, literally.

We passed through the bubble, which was like a thin film of dense water. My entire body received a high voltage shock. An electrical current ran through me from my head to the end of my toes. "*I am beginning to remember.*" I communicated to Zenix, who just gave me an odd smirk.

I realized we were no longer swimming in water, but floating toward a grand silver palace. The palace was ornate and majestic. Towers that stretched to the top of the force field bubble decorated its corners. I was in awe.

"*Remember Kyle, remember.*" I was feeling a sense of urgency now. There was something not quite right.

Once our feet landed on the firm granite-like floor, Zenix walked me through a set of beautifully crafted, gigantic doors. At the end of a room lined with pillars, which looked like a cathedral I read about in a book of Roger's, sat a beautiful, crowned woman on a golden throne. She must be our queen.

Was this the woman from my dreams? The one whose voice gave me the strength and courage to heal Big Mike?

I continued to follow Zenix. The woman spotted us and she stood up. I smiled, anticipating a jubilant reunion. Black Hair and Blondie emerged from behind a pillar. There was not a scratch on them. My smile quickly faded and I stopped and stood frozen. Alive? Or was I now dead?

I turned to Zenix for an explanation. Without warning, he snapped what the land folk would have called "handcuffs" onto my wrists. The bracelets were not made from metal though, they were formed from an effervescent liquid.

"What's happening?" I shouted, using my real voice. Zenix stepped away from me and at least a dozen guards armed with spears formed a tight circle around me.

"Welcome home, brother." Zenix sneered.

All heads turned as the queen pointed at me and in the Atlantean language commanded. "Bring the prisoner forward."

Yes, unfortunately now my familiarity of our language came back to me. My eyes filled with tears as my memory began to unlock. "*Kyle Roger Starr*," I thought, "*what did you do?*"

Who I was and what I'd done all came painfully flooding back to me. I remembered everything, and it was not good, not good at all.

The End…For Now

About the Author

Knight Jordan has a Masters in Organizational Management from the University of Phoenix and a Bachelor's in Theater and Film from Brigham Young University. Knight Jordan loves movies and superheroes. He enjoys watching and participating in boxing, basketball, and hockey. One of his favorite quotes is, "Treat an individual as he is, he will remain how he is, but if you treat him as he ought to be, he will become as he ought to be and could be." Goethe. Knight is a former Canadian, now living with his beautiful wife and amazing children in scenic Utah.

www.ingramcontent.com/pod-product-compliance
Lightning Source LLC
Chambersburg PA
CBHW061538170626
46811CB00001B/21